Tom Ossington's Ghost by Richard Marsh

Richard Bernard Heldmann was born on 12th October 1857, in St Johns Wood, North London.

By his early 20's Heldmann began publishing fiction for the myriad magazine publications that had sprung up and were eager for good well-written content.

In October 1882, Heldmann was promoted to co-editor of Union Jack, a popular magazine, but his association with the publication ended suddenly in June 1883. It appears Heldman was prone to issuing forged cheques to finance his lifestyle. In April 1884 He was sentenced to 18 months hard labour.

In order to be well away from the scandal and damage this had caused to his reputation Heldmann adopted a pseudonym on his release from jail. Shortly thereafter the name 'Richard Marsh' began to appear in the literary periodicals. The use of his mother's maiden name as part of it seems both a release and a lifeline.

A stroke of very good fortune arrived with his novel The Beetle published in 1897. This would turn out to be his greatest commercial success and added some much-needed gravitas to his literary reputation.

Marsh was a prolific writer and wrote almost 80 volumes of fiction as well as many short stories, across many genres from horror and crime to romance and humour.

Index of Contents

The first of the series of curious happenings, which led to such a surprising and, indeed, extraordinary denouement, occurred on the twelfth of October. It was a Monday; about four-thirty in the afternoon. Madge Brodie was alone in the house. The weather was dull, a suspicion of mist was in the air, already the day was drawing in.

Madge was writing away with might and main, hard at work on one of those MSS. with which she took such peculiar pains; and with which the editors for whom they were destined took so little. If they would only take a little more—enough to read them through, say—Madge felt sure they would not be so continually returned. Her pen went tearing away at a gallop—it had reached the last few lines—they were finished. She turned to glance at the clock which was on the mantelshelf behind her.

"Gracious!—I had no idea it was so late. Ella will be home in an hour, and there is nothing in the place for her to eat!"

She caught up the sheets of paper, fastened them together at the corner, crammed them into an envelope, scribbled a note, crammed it in after them, addressed the envelope, closed it, jumped up to get her hat, just as there came a rat-tat-tat at the hall-door knocker.

"Now, who's that? I wonder if it is that Miss Brice come for her lesson after all—three hours late. It will be like her if it is—but she sha'n't have it now. We'll see if she shall."

She caught up her hat from the couch, perched it on her head, pushed a pin through the crown.

"If she sees that I am just going out, I should think that even she will hardly venture to ask me to give her a lesson three hours after the time which she herself appointed."

As she spoke she was crossing the little passage towards the front door.

It was not Miss Brice—it was a man. A man, too, who behaved somewhat oddly. No sooner had Madge opened the door, than stepping into the tiny hall, without waiting for any sort of invitation, taking the handle from her hand, he shut it after him with considerably more haste than ceremony. She stared, while he leaned against the wall as if he was short of breath.

He was tall; she only reached to his shoulder, and she was scarcely short. He was young—there was not a hair on his face. He was dressed in blue serge, and when he removed his felt hat he disclosed a well-shaped head covered with black hair, cut very short, with the apparent intention of getting the better of its evident tendency to curl at the tips. His marked feature, at that moment, was his obvious discomposure. He did not look as if he was a nervous sort of person; yet, just then, the most bashful bumpkin could not have seemed more ill at ease. Madge was at a loss what to make of him.

"I'm feeling a little faint."

The words were stammered out, as if with a view of explaining the singularity of his bearing—yet he did not appear to be the kind of individual who might be expected to feel "a little faint," unless nature belied her own handwriting. The strength and constitution of a Samson was written large all over him. It seemed to strike him that his explanation—such as it was—was a little lame, so he stammered something else.

"You give music lessons?"

"Yes, we do give music lessons—at least, I do."

"You? Oh!—You do?"

His tone implied—or seemed to imply—that her appearance was hardly consistent with that of a giver of music lessons. She drew herself a little up.

"I do give music lessons. Have you been recommended by one of my pupils?"

She cast her mind over the scanty list to ascertain which of them might be likely to give such a recommendation. His stumbling answer saved her further trouble on that score.

"No, I—I saw the plate on the gate, so I—I thought I'd just come in and ask you to give me one."

"Give you a music lesson?"

"Yes, if you wouldn't mind."

"But"—she paused, hardly knowing what to say. She had never contemplated giving lessons to pupils of this description. "I never have given lessons to a—gentleman. I supposed they always went to professors of their own sex."

"Do they? I don't know. I hope you don't mind making an exception in my case. I—I'm so fond of music." Suddenly he changed the subject. "This is Clover Cottage?"

"Yes, this is Clover Cottage."

"Are you—pardon me—but are you Miss Ossington?"

"Ossington? No—that is not my name."

"But doesn't some one of that name live here?"

"No one. I never heard it before. I think there must be some mistake."

She laid her hand on the latch—by way of giving him a hint to go. He prevented her opening it, placing his own hand against the door; courteously, yet unmistakably.

"Excuse me—but I hope you will give me a lesson; if it is only of a quarter of an hour, to try what I can do—to see if it would be worth your while to have me as a pupil. I have been long looking for an opportunity of taking lessons, and when I saw your plate on the gate I jumped at the chance."

She hesitated. The situation was an odd one—and yet she had already been for some time aware that young women who are fighting for daily bread have not seldom to face odd situations. Funds were desperately low. She had to contribute her share to the expenses of the little household, and that share was in arrear. Of late MSS. had been coming back more monotonously than ever. Pupils—especially those who were willing to pay possible prices—were few and far between. Who was she, that she should turn custom from the door? It was nothing that this was a stranger—all her pupils were strangers at the beginning; most of them were still strangers at the end. Men, she had heard, pay better than women. She might take advantage of this person's sex to charge him extra terms—even to the extent of five shillings a lesson instead of half a crown. It was an opportunity she could not afford to lose. She resolved to at least go so far as to learn exactly what it was he wanted; and then if, from any point of view, it seemed advisable, to make an appointment for a future date.

She led the way into the sitting room—he following.

"Are you quite a beginner?" she asked.

"No, not—not altogether."

"Let me see what you can do."

She went to a pile of music which was on a little table, for the purpose of selecting a piece of sufficient simplicity to enable a tyro to display his powers, or want of them. He was between her and the window. In passing the window he glanced through it. As he did so, he gave a sudden start—a start, in fact, which amounted to a positive jump. His hat dropped from his hand, and, wholly regardless that he was leaving it lying on the floor, he hurried backwards, keeping in the shadow, and as far as possible from the window. The action was so marked that it was impossible it should go unnoticed. It filled Madge Brodie with a sense of shock which was distinctly disagreeable. Her eyes, too, sought the window—it looked out on to the road. A man, it struck her, of emphatically sinister appearance, was loitering leisurely past. As she looked he stopped dead, and, leaning over the palings, stared intently through the window. It was true that the survey only lasted for a moment, and that then he shambled off again, but the thing was sufficiently conspicuous to be unpleasant.

So startled was she by the connection which seemed to exist between the fellow's insolence and her visitor's perturbation that, without thinking of what she was doing, she placed the first piece she came across upon the music-stand—saying, as she did so:

"Let me see what you can do with this."

Her words were unheeded. Her visitor was drawing himself into an extreme corner of the room, in a fashion which, considering his size and the muscle which his appearance suggested, was, in its way, ludicrous. It was not, however, the ludicrous side which occurred to Madge; his uneasiness made her uneasy too. She spoke a little sharply, as if involuntarily.

"Do you hear me? Will you be so good as to try this piece, and let me see what you can make of it."

Her words seemed to rouse him to a sense of misbehaviour.

"I beg your pardon; I am afraid you will think me rude, but the truth is, I—I have been a little out of sorts just lately." He came briskly towards the piano; glancing however, as Madge could not help but notice, nervously through the window as he came. The man outside was gone; his absence seemed to reassure him. "Is this the piece you wish me to play? I will do my best."

He did his best—or, if it was not his best, his best must have been something very remarkable indeed.

The piece she had selected—unwittingly—was a Minuet of Mozart's. A dainty trifle; a pitfall for the inexperienced; seeming so simple, yet needing the soul, and knowledge, of a virtuoso to make anything of it at all. Hardly the sort of thing to set before a seeker after music lessons, whose acquaintance with music, for all she knew, was limited to picking out the notes upon the keyboard. At her final examination she herself had chosen it, first because she loved it, and, second, because she deemed it to be something which would enable her to illustrate her utmost powers at their very best.

It was only when he struck the first few notes that she realised what it was she had put in front of him; when she did, she was startled. Whether he understood what the piece was there for—that he was being set to play it as an exhibition of his ignorance rather than of his knowledge—was difficult to say. It is quite possible that in the preoccupation of his mind it had escaped him altogether that the sole excuse for his presence in that room lay in the fact that he was seeking lessons from this young girl. There could be no doubt whatever that at least one of the things that he had said of himself was true, and that he did love music; there could be just as little doubt that he already was a musician of a quite unusual calibre—one who had been both born and made.

He played the delicate fragment with an exquisite art which filled Madge Brodie with amazement. She had never heard it played like that before—never! Not even by her own professor. Perhaps her surprise was so great that, in the first flush of it, she exaggerated the player's powers.

It seemed to her that this man played like one who saw into the very depths of the composer's soul, and who had all the highest resources of his art at his command to enable him to give a perfect—an ideal—rendering. Such an exquisite touch! such masterly fingering! such wondrous phrasing! such light and shade! such insight and such execution! She had not supposed that her cheap piano had been capable of such celestial harmony. She listened spellbound—for she, too, had imagination, and she, too, loved music. All was forgotten in the moment's rapture—in her delight at hearing so unexpectedly sounding in her ears, what seemed to her, in her excitement, the very music of the spheres. The player seemed to be as oblivious of his surroundings as Madge Brodie—his very being seemed wrapped up in the ecstasy of producing the quaint, sweet music for the stately old-time measure.

When he had finished, the couple came back to earth, with a rush.

With an apparent burst of recollection his hands came off the keyboard, and he wheeled round upon the music-stool with an air of conscience-stricken guilt. Madge stood close by, actually quivering with a conflict of emotions. He met her eyes—instantly to avert his own. There was silence—then a slight tremor in her voice in spite of her effort to prevent it.

"I suppose you have been having a little jest at my expense."

"A jest at your expense?"

"I daresay that is what you call it—though I believe in questions of humour there is room for wide differences of opinion. I should call it something else."

"I don't understand you."

"That is false."

At this point-blank contradiction, the blood showed through his sallow cheeks.

"False?"

"Yes, false. You do understand me. Did you not say that you had been for some time seeking for an opportunity to take lessons in music?"

"I—I—"

Confronted by her red-hot accusatory glances, he stammered, stumbled, stopped.

"Yes?—go on."

"I have been seeking such an opportunity."

"Indeed? And do you wish me to suppose that you believed that you—you—could be taught anything in music by an unknown creature who fastened a plate announcing lessons in music, to the palings of such a place as this?"

He was silent—looking as if he would have spoken, but could not. She went on:

"I thank you for the pleasure you have given me—the unexpected pleasure. It is a favourite piece of mine which you have just performed—I say 'performed' advisedly. I never heard it better played by any one—never! and I never shall. You are a great musician. I?—I am a poor teacher of the rudiments of the art in which you are such an adept. I am obliged by your suggestion that I should give you lessons. I regret that to do so is out of my power. You already play a thousand times better than I ever shall—I was just going out as you came in. I must ask you to be so good as to permit me to go now."

He rose from the music stool—towering above her higher and higher. From his altitude he looked down at her for some seconds in silence. Then, in his deep bass voice, he began, as it seemed, to excuse himself.

"Believe me—"

She cut him short.

"I believe nothing—and wish to believe nothing. You had reasons of your own for coming here; what they were I do not know, nor do I seek to know. All I desire is that you should take yourself away."

He stooped to pick up his hat. Rising with it in his hand, he glanced towards the window. As he did so, the man who had leaned over the palings came strolling by again. The sight of this man filled him with his former uneasiness. He retreated further back into the room—all but stumbling over Miss Brodie in his haste. In a person of his physique the agitation he displayed was pitiful. It suggested a degree of cowardice which nothing in his appearance seemed to warrant.

"I—I beg your pardon—but might I ask you a favour?"

"A favour? What is it?"

"I will be frank with you. I am being watched by a person whose scrutiny I wish to avoid. Because I wished to escape him was one reason why I came in here."

Madge went to the window. The man in the road was lounging lazily along with an air of indifference which was almost too marked to be real. He gave a backward glance as he went. At sight of Madge he quickened his pace.

"Is that the man who is watching you?"

"Yes, I—I fancy it is."

"You fancy? Don't you know?"

"It is the man."

"He is shorter than you—smaller altogether. Compared to you he is a dwarf. Why are you afraid of him?"

Either the question itself, or the tone in which it was asked, brought the blood back into his cheeks.

"I did not say I was afraid."

"No? Then if you are not afraid, why should you have been so anxious to avoid him as to seek refuge, on so shallow a pretext, in a stranger's house?"

The intruder bit his lip. His manner was sullen.

"I regret that the circumstances which have brought me here are of so singular and complicated a character as to prevent my giving you the full explanation to which you may consider yourself entitled. I am sorry that I should have sought refuge beneath your roof as I own I did; and the more so as I am compelled to ask you another favour—permission to leave that refuge by means of the back door."

She twirled round on her heels and faced him.

"The back door!"

"I presume there is a back door?"

"Certainly—only it leads to the front."

Again he bit his lip. His temper did not seem to be improving. The girl's tone, face, bearing, were instinct with scorn.

"Is there no means of getting away by the back without returning to the front?"

"Only by climbing a hedge and a fence on to the common."

"Perhaps the feat will be within my powers—if you will allow me to try."

"Allow you to try! And is it possible that you forced your way into the house on the pretence of seeking lessons in music, when your real motive was to seek an opportunity of evading pursuit by means of the back door?"

"I am aware that the seeming anomaly of my conduct entitles you to think the worst of me."

"Seeming anomaly!" She laughed contemptuously. "Pray, sir, permit me to lead the way—to the back door."

She strode off, with her head in the air; he came after, with a brow as black as night. At the back door they paused.

"I thank you for having afforded me shelter, and apologise for having sought it."

She looked him up and down, as if she were endeavouring, by mere force of visual inspection, to make out what kind of a man he was.

"I want to ask you a question. Answer it truthfully, if you can. Is the man in front a policeman?"

He started with what seemed genuine surprise.

"A policeman! Good heavens, no."

"Are you sure?"

"Of course I'm sure. He's very far from being a policeman—rather, if anything, the other way." What he meant to infer, she did not know; but he laughed shortly, "What makes you ask such a thing?"

She was holding the door open in her hand. He had crossed the threshold and stood without. Malice—and something else—gleamed in her eyes.

"Because," she answered, "I wondered if you were a thief."

With that she slammed the door in his face and turned the key. Then, slipping into the kitchen which was on her left, keeping the door on the jar, remaining well in the shadow, she watched his proceedings through the window.

For a moment he stayed where she had left him standing, as if rooted to the spot. Then, with an exaggerated courtesy, taking off his hat, he bowed to the door. Turning, he marched down the garden path, his tall figure seeming more gigantic than ever as she noted how straight he held himself. In a twinkling he was over the fence and hedge. Once on the other side, he shook his fist at Clover Cottage.

The watcher in the kitchen clenched her teeth as she perceived the gesture.

"Ungrateful creature! And to think that a man who has the very spirit of music in his soul, and who plays the piano like an angel, should be such a wretch! That a monster seven feet high, who looks like a combination of Samson and Goliath rolled into one, should be such a coward and a cur—afraid of a pigmy five foot high! I hope I've seen the last of him. If I have any more such pupils I shall have to shut up shop. Now perhaps I shall be allowed to post my MS. and run across to Brown's to get a chop for Ella's tea."

With that she passed from the back to the front. Outside the front door she paused to look around her and take her bearings, half doubtful as to whether any more dubious strangers might not be in sight.

The only person to be seen was the man whose presence had proved so disconcerting to her recent visitor. He had reached the corner of the street, and, turning, strolled slowly back towards Clover Cottage. He gave one quick, shifty glance at her as she came out, but beyond that he took—or appeared to take—no notice of her appearance.

"Now, I wonder," she said to herself, "who you may be. Your friend, who, for all I know, is now running for his life across the common, said you were no policeman—and, I am bound to say, you don't look as if you were; he added that, if anything, you were rather the other way. If, by that, he meant you were a thief, I'm free to admit you look your profession to the life. I wonder if it would be safe to run across to Brown's while you're about;—not that I'm afraid of you, as I'll prove to your entire satisfaction if you only let me have the chance. Only you seem to be one of those agreeable creatures who, f they are only sure that a house is empty, and there's not even a girl inside, can enact to perfection the part of area sneak; and neither Ella nor I wish to lose any of the few possessions which we have."

While she hesitated a curious scene took place—a scene in which the gentleman on the prowl played a leading rôle.

The road in which Clover Cottage stood was bisected on the right and left by other streets, within a hundred yards of the house itself. On reaching the corner of the street on the left, the gentleman on the prowl, as we have seen, had performed a right-about-face, and returned to the cottage. As he advanced, a woman came round the corner of the street, upon the right. He saw her the instant she appeared, and the sight had on him an astonishing effect. He stopped, as if petrified; stared, as if the eyes were starting from his head; gave a great gasp; turned; tore off like a hunted animal; dashed round the corner on the left; and vanished out of sight. Having advanced to within a few feet of where Madge was standing, she was a close spectator of his singular behaviour. As she looked to see what had been the exciting cause, half expecting that her recent visitor had come back and that the tables had been turned, and the gentleman on the prowl had played the coward in his turn, the woman who had come round the other corner had already reached the cottage. Pushing the gate unceremoniously open, she strode straight past Madge, and, without a with-your-leave or by-your-leave, marched through the open door into the hall beyond.

As Madge eyed her with mingled surprise and indignation she exclaimed, with what seemed unnecessary ferocity—

"I've come to see the house."

CHAPTER II

THERE'S A CONSCIENCE!

Madge had been taken so wholly unawares that for a moment she remained stock-still—and voiceless. Then she followed the woman to the door.

"You have come to do what?"

"I've come to see the house."

"And pray who are you?"

"What affair is that of yours? Don't I tell you I've come to see the house?"

"But I don't understand you. What do you mean by saying you've come to see the house?"

For only answer the woman, turning her back on her, walked another step or two along the little passage. She exclaimed, as if addressing the staircase, which was in front of her, in what seemed a tone of intense emotion—

"How his presence is in all the place! How he fills the air!"

Madge felt more bewildered than she would have cared to admit. Was the woman mad? Mad or sane, she resolved that she would not submit tamely to such another irruption as the last. She laid her hand upon the woman's shoulder.

"Will you be so good as to tell me, at once, to whom I have the pleasure of speaking, and what business has brought you here?"

The woman turned and looked at her; as she did so, Madge was conscious of a curious sense of discomfort.

She was of medium height, slender build, and apparently between forty and fifty years of age. Her attire was not only shabby, it was tawdry to the last degree. Her garments were a heterogeneous lot; one might safely swear they had none of them been made for the wearer. One and all were shocking examples of outworn finery. The black chip hat which she wore perched on her head, with an indescribable sort of would-be jauntiness, was broken at the brim, and the one-time gorgeous ostrich feathers were crushed and soiled. A once well-cut cape of erstwhile dark blue cloth was about her shoulders. It was faded, stained, and creased. The fur which had been used to adorn the edges was bare and rusty. It had been lined with silk—as she moved her arms one perceived that of the lining there was nothing left but rags and tatters. Her dress, once the latest fashionable freak in some light-hued flimsy silk, had long since been fit for nothing else than cutting into dusters. She wore ancient patent-leather shoes upon her feet, and equally ancient gloves upon her hands—the bare flesh showing through holes in every finger.

If her costume was strange, her face was stranger. It was the face of a woman who had once been beautiful—how long ago, no one who chanced on her haphazard could with any certainty have guessed. It might have been five, ten, fifteen, twenty years ago—and more than that—since hers had been a countenance which charmed even a casual beholder. It was the face of a woman who had been weak or wicked, and maybe both, and who in consequence had been bandied from pillar to post, till this was all that there was left of her. Her big blue eyes were deep set in careworn caverns; her mouth, which had once been small and dainty, was now blurred and pendulous, the mouth of a woman who drank; her cheeks were sunk and hollow as if she had lost every tooth in her head, the cheek-bones gleaming through the yellow skin in sharp and cruel ridges. To crown it all, her hair was dyed—a vivid yellow. Like all the rest of her, the dye was old and worn. It stood in urgent need of a renewal. The roots were grey, they demonstrated their greyness with savage ostentation. Here and there among the yellow there were grey patches too—in some queer way her attempt at juvenescence had made her look older even than she was.

This was not a pleasant face to have encountered anywhere at any time, being the sort from which good women instinctively shrink back. Just now its unpleasantness was intensified by the fact that it was lit up by some, to Madge, inscrutable emotion; inflamed by some mastering excitement. The hollow eyes gleamed as if they were lighted by inner fires; the lips twitched as if the muscles which worked them were uncontrollable. The woman spoke in short, sharp, angry gusts, as if she were stumbling on the verge of frenzied passion.

"This house is mine," she said.

"Yours?"

"It was his, and mine—and now it's mine."

Madge, persuaded that the woman must be either mad or drunk, felt that perhaps calmness might be her safest weapon.

"Do you mean that you're the landlady?"

"The landlady!" The woman laughed—unmirthfully. "There is no landlady. And the landlord—he's a ghost. He's in it now—don't you feel that he is in it?"

She spoke with such singular intensity that, in spite of herself, Madge shuddered. She was feeling more and more uncomfortable—wishing heartily that some one might come, if it was only the mysterious stranger who had previously intruded.

The woman went on—her excitement seeming to grow with every word she uttered.

"The house is full of ghosts—full! They're in every corner, every nook and cranny—and I know them every one. Come here—I'll show you some of them."

She caught the girl by the arm. Madge, yielding to her strange frenzy, suffered herself to be led into the sitting-room. Once inside, the woman loosed her hold. She looked about her. Then crossed to the fireplace, standing in the centre of the hearthrug.

"This is where I struck him." She pointed just in front of her. "He was sitting there. I had asked him for some money. He would not let me have any. He always clung to his money—always! I swear it— always!" She raised her hands, as if appealing to the ceiling to bear her witness. "He said that I was ruining him. Ruining him? bah! I knew better than that. He would let no one ruin him—he was not of that kind. I told him I must have money. He said he'd given me five pounds last week. 'Five pounds!' I cried; 'what are five pounds?' Then we quarrelled—he said things, I said things. Then I flew into a rage; my temper has been the curse of my whole life. I caught up a decanter of whisky which was on the table, and struck him with it on the head. The bottle broke, the whisky went all over him—how it smelt! Can't you smell it?—and he went tumbling down, down, on to the floor. He's lying there now—can't you see him lying there?" She turned to Madge with a gesture which seemed to make the girl's blood run colder. "Can't you see the ghost?"

She moved a little to one side.

"Just here is where I knelt down, and asked him to forgive me. That was after—I'd been carrying on with some fellow I'd met at a dance, and he had found me out. I cried and cried as if my heart would break, and at last he came and put his hand upon my head—when I set myself to do it, and stuck at it, I could twist him round my finger!—and he began to stroke my hair—I'd lovely hair then, no woman ever had lovelier, and he was always one to stroke it when I'd let him!—and he said, 'My girl, how often shall I have to forgive you?' Listen! Can't you hear him saying it now? Can't you see the ghost?"

She went to where the modest sideboard stood.

"This is where we had our sideboard too—it was a bigger one than this; all our things were good. I was standing here, leaning against it just like this, the first time he saw me drunk. He'd been out all the evening on some sort of business, and I'd been left in the house alone with the girl, and I hadn't liked it, and I'd been sulking. And at last I got to the whisky and I started to drink, drink, drink. I always had been fond of drink long before that, but I'd never let him find it out. But that time I was that sulky I didn't seem to care, and by the time I might have cared I couldn't care—I was too far gone. I had to keep on drinking. There wasn't much in the bottle; when I got to the end of it I started on another. Then I got to the sideboard, and stood leaning over it, lolly fashion, booze, booze, boozing. All of a sudden the door opened, and he came into the room. I turned to have a look at him, the bottle in one hand and the glass in the other. Directly I got clear of the sideboard I went flop on the floor, and the bottle and the glass went with me, and there I had to lie. He rushed towards me, and as soon as he had had a look at me he saw how it was. Then he fell on his knees at my side, and put his hands up to his face, and began to cry. My God, how he did cry!—not like me. His sobs seemed tearing him to pieces, and his life's blood seemed coming from him with every tear. Drunk as I was, it made me cry to hear him. Listen! Can't you hear him crying now? Can't you see the ghost?"

The woman's words and manner were so realistic, and despite—or perhaps because of—her seeming frenzy, she had such an eerie capacity of conjuring up the picture as her memory painted it, that Madge listened spellbound. She was as incapable of interrupting the other's flow of language as if the conscience haunted wretch had cast on her some strange enchantment.

The sea of visions went to the table, and, bending over it, beckoned to Madge to draw closer. As if she found the invitation irresistible, Madge approached. The woman's outstretched finger pointed to a particular place about the centre of one side of the table. Her excitement all at once subsided; her voice grew softer. Her manner became more human, more womanly.

"See!—this is where my little baby died—my little child—the only one I ever had. It was a girl; we called it Lily—my name's Lily"—she glanced up with a grin, as if conscious of how grotesquely inappropriate, in her case, such a name was now; "it was such a little thing—I didn't want it when it came. I never was fond of children, and I wasn't one to play the mother. But, when it did come, it got hold of me somehow—yes, it did! it did! I was fond of it, in my way. As for him, he worshipped it; it was baby, baby, baby! all the time. I was nowhere. It made me wild to hear him, and to see the way that he went on. We fell out because I would have it brought up by hand. He wanted me to let it have my milk—but I wouldn't have it. I wasn't going to be any baby's slave—not likely! I don't think he ever forgave me that. Then he was always at me because he said I neglected it; and that made me worse than ever: I wasn't going to have a crying brat thrust down my throat at every turn, and so I told him. 'Why isn't there a place in which they bring up babies so that they needn't worry their mothers?' I wanted to know. When I said that, how he did look at me, and how he went on! I thought he would have killed me—but I didn't care. He did his share of all the nursing that baby ever had—and perhaps a little more."

Again the woman laughed.

"At last the little thing went wrong. It always was small; it never seemed to grow—except thin. It was the queerest looking little mite, with a serious face like a parson's, and great big eyes which seemed to go right through you, as if it was looking at something which nobody but itself could see. He would have it that it got worse and worse, but he was always making such a fuss that I said he was making a fool of the child. The doctor came and came, but I was pretty often out, and when I wasn't I didn't always choose to see him, so I only heard what he cared to tell me—and I didn't believe the half of that.

"One night I went to a masked ball with Mrs. Sutton—she was a larky one, she was, and led her husband a pretty dance. It was latish when I came back; I hadn't enjoyed myself one bit, and left in a temper and came off home by myself I let myself in at the front door, and when I came into this room, on the table just here"—she pointed with her finger—"there was a pillow, and on the pillow was the baby, and he was kneeling on the floor in front, his elbows on the table, and his face on his hands, and the tears streaming down his cheeks as if they'd never stop. I'd been to the ball as a ballet girl—though he hadn't known it, and I hadn't meant that he should, but the sight took me so aback that, without thinking, I dropped my cloak and stood before him just as I was. 'What's the matter now?' I cried; 'what's the child down here at this time of the night for?' I expected that he'd let fly at me, and perhaps send me packing out of the house right there and then. But, instead, he just glanced my way as if he hardly saw me, or wanted to, and said, 'Baby's dying.' When he said that, it was as if he had run something right into my heart. 'Dying,' I cried, 'stuff!' I ran to the table and bent over the pillow. I had never seen anybody dying before, and knew nothing at all about it, but directly I looked at it, I seemed to know that what he said was true, and that the child was dying. My heart stopped beating—I couldn't breathe, I couldn't speak, I couldn't move, I could only stare like a creature who had lost her wits—it was as if a hand had been stretched right out of Heaven to strike me a blow. There he was on one side of the table—and there was me leaning right over the other, both of us motionless, neither of us speaking a word; and there was the baby lying on the pillow between us, stiller than we were. How long we stopped like that I don't know; it seemed to me as if it was hours—but I daresay it was only a few minutes. All at once the baby—my baby—gave a little movement with its little arms—a sort of trembling. He moved his arm, and put one of his fingers into its tiny hand; the baby seemed to fasten on to it. 'Give it one of your fingers,' he said, sobbing as if his heart would break. 'It'll like to feel your finger as it goes!' Hardly knowing what I was doing, I stretched out one of my fingers; it was the first finger of my right hand—this one." She held up the finger in question in its ragged casing. "And I put it in the mite's wee hand. It took it—yes, it took it. It closed its fingers right round it, and gave it quite a squeeze—yes, quite a squeeze. Then it loosened its hold. It was dead. Dead upon the pillow.—And it's there now. Can't you see it lying on the pillow, with a smile on its face? a smile! Can't you see the ghost?"

Stooping, the woman made pretence to kiss the lips of some one who was lying just beneath her. It might have been that to her the thing was no pretence, and that, as in a vision, the dead lips did indeed touch hers. Then, drawing herself erect again, she broke into another of her discordant laughs. Throwing out her arms on either side of her, she exclaimed in strident tones:

"Ghosts! Ghosts! The place is full of them—I see them everywhere. I touch them, hear them all the time. They've been with me all through the years, wherever I've been—and where haven't I been? My God— in heaven and hell! crowds and crowds of them, more and more as the years went on. And do you think that I can't see them here—in their house, and mine! Can't you see them too?"

Madge replied between set lips—she had been forming her own conclusions while the woman raved:

"No, I do not see them. Nor would you were you not under the influence of drink."

The woman stared at her in what seemed genuine surprise.

"Under the influence of drink! Me? No such luck! I wish I were." Again she gave one of those bursts of laughter which so jarred on Madge's nerves. "When I'm drunk I can't see ghosts—it's only when I'm sober. I've had nothing to eat since I don't know when, let alone to drink. I'm starving, starving! That's the time when I see ghosts. They point at me with their fingers and say, 'Look at us and look at you—this is what it's come to!' They make me see what might have been. He made me come to-day; I didn't want to, but he made me. And now he's in all the house.—Listen! He's getting out of bed in the room upstairs—that's his bedroom. Can't you hear his lame foot moving about the floor? How often I've thrown that lame foot in his face when I've been wild!—can't you hear it hobble—hobble?"

"You are mad! How dare you talk such nonsense? There's no one in the house but you and I."

The woman seemed to believe so implicitly in the diseased imaginings of her conscience-haunted brain, that Madge felt that unless she made a resolute effort her own mental equilibrium might totter. On the other's face there came a look of shrewd, malignant cunning.

"Isn't there! That's all you know,—I'm no more mad than you are. And I tell you what—he's not the only thing that's in the house. There's something else as well. It was his, and now it's mine. And don't you think to rob me."

"Rob you?—I."

"Yes, you. There's others after it as well as you—I know! I'm not the simpleton that some may think. But I won't be robbed by all the lot of you—you make no error. It was his, and now it's mine."

"If there really is anything in the house to which you have the slightest shadow of a claim, which I very much doubt, and let me know what it is, and where it is, I'll see that you have it without fail."

A look of vacancy came on the woman's face. She passed her hand across her brow.

"That's it—I don't know just where it is. He comes and tells me, almost, but never quite. He says it's in the house, but he doesn't say exactly where. But he never lies—so I do know it's in the house, and I won't be robbed."

"I have not the slightest idea of what you mean—if you really do mean anything at all. I don't know if you know me—or are under the impression that I know you; if so, I can only assure you that I don't. I have not the faintest notion who you are."

The woman, drawing nearer, clutched Madge's arm with both her hands.

"Don't you know who I am? I'm the ghost's wife!"

Her manner was not only exceedingly unpleasant; it was, in a sense, uncanny—so uncanny that, in spite of herself, Madge could not help a startled look coming into her face. The appearance of this look seemed to amuse her tormentor. She broke into a continuous peal of unmelodious laughter.

"I'm the ghost's wife!" she kept repeating. "I'm the ghost's wife."

Madge Brodie prided herself on her strength of nerve, and as, a rule, not without cause. But, on that occasion, almost for the first time in her life it played her false. She would have been glad to have been able to scream and flee; but she was incapable even of doing that. The other seemed to hold her spellbound; she was conscious that her senses were reeling—that, unless something happened soon, she would faint.

But from that final degradation she was saved.

"Madge," exclaimed a voice, "who is this woman?"

It was Ella Duncan, and with her was Jack Martyn. At the sound of the voice, the woman released her hold. Never before had Madge been sensible of such a spasm of relief. She rushed to Ella with a hysterical sob.

"Oh, Ella!" she cried, "how thankful I am you've come."

Ella looked at her with surprise.

"Madge!—who is this woman?"

The woman in question spoke for herself. She threw up her arms.

"I'm the ghost's wife!" she shrieked, "I'm the ghost's wife!"

Before they had suspected her purpose, or could say anything to stop her, she had rushed out of the room and from the house.

CHAPTER III

TWO LONE, LORN YOUNG WOMEN

Ella and Jack eyed each other. Madge took refuge in a chair, conscious of a feeling of irritation at her weakness now that the provocation had passed. Ella regarded her curiously.

"What's the matter with you, Madge? What's happened?"

"It's nothing—only that horrible woman has upset me."

"Who is she? and what's she been doing? and what's she want?"

"I don't know who she is, or what she wants, or anything at all about her. I only know that she's prevented me getting anything for your tea."

"That's all right—we've got something, haven't we, Jack?" Jack waved a parcel. "But whatever did you let such an extraordinary-looking creature into the house for? and whatever did she mean by screaming out that she's a ghost's wife? Is she very mad?"

"I think she is—and I didn't let her in."

Then, while they were preparing tea, the tale was told, or at least a part of it. But even that part was enough to make Jack Martyn grave. As the telling proceeded, he grew graver and graver, until, at the end, he wore a face of portentous gloom. When they seated themselves to the meal he made precisely the remark which they had expected him to make. He rested his hands on his knees, and he solemnly shook his head.

"This comes of your being alone in the house!"

Ella laughed.

"There! now you've started him on his own particular crotchet; he'll never let you hear the last of this."

Jack went on.

"I've said before, and I say again, and I shall keep on saying, that you two girls ought not to live alone by yourselves in a house in this out-of-the-way corner of the world."

"Out-of-the-way corner of the world!—on Wandsworth Common!"

"For all practical intents and purposes you might as well be in the middle of the Desert of Sahara; you might shriek and shriek and I doubt if any one would hear you. This agreeable visitor of Madge's might have cut her throat from ear to ear, or chopped her into mincemeat, and she would have been as incapable of summoning assistance as if she had been at the top of Mont Blanc."

"That's it. Jack—pile it on!"

"I don't think it's fair of you to talk like that, Ella; I'm not piling it on; I'm just speaking the plain and simple truth. Honestly, Madge, when you've been alone in the house all day long, haven't you felt that you were at the mercy of the first evil-disposed person who chose to come along; or, if you haven't felt it before, don't you think you'll feel it now?"

"No—to both your questions."

"Supposing this woman comes back again to-morrow?"

Madge had to bite her lip to repress a shudder; the idea was not a pleasant one.

"She won't come back."

"But suppose she does?—and from what you say I think it very probable that she will; if not to-morrow, then the day after."

"If she comes the day after to-morrow she'll find me out; I shall be out all day."

"There's a confession! It's only because you know that you will be out that you're able to face the prospect with equanimity."

"You are not entitled to infer anything of the kind."

Ella interposed, perceiving that the girl was made uncomfortable by the man's persistence.

"Don't do quite so much supposing, Jack; let me do a little for a change. Suppose we lived in one of those flats in the charming neighbourhood of Chancery Lane or Bloomsbury, after which—vicariously—your soul so hankers, how much better off should we be there?"

"You would, at any rate, be within the reach of assistance."

"No more so than we are now, because, quite probably, the kind of neighbours we should be likely to have in the sort of flat we should be able to afford would be worse—much worse—than none at all. The truth is that two lonely, hard-up girls—desperately hard-up girls—will be lonely wherever they are. We are quite prepared for that. Only we intend to choose the particular kind of loneliness which we happen to prefer—don't we, Madge?"

"Of course we do."

"It makes me wild to hear you say such things. Rather than you should feel like that, I'd marry on nothing."

"Thank you, but I wouldn't. I find it quite hard enough to be single on nothing."

"You know what I mean; I don't mean actually on nothing. I was reckoning it up the other night. My income—"

"Your income's like mine, Jack—capable of considerable increment. And would you be so kind as to change the subject?"

But the thing was easier said than done. Jack's thoughts had been started in a groove, and they kept in it; the conversation was continually reverting to the subject of the girls' loneliness. His last words as he left the room were on the familiar theme.

"I grant that there are advantages in having a pretty little place like this all to yourselves, especially when you get it at a peppercorn rent; and that it's nice to be your own mistresses, and all that kind of thing. But in the case of you two girls the disadvantages are so many and so serious, that I wonder you don't see them more clearly for yourselves. Anyhow, Madge has had her first peep at them to-day, and I sincerely hope it will be her last; though I am persuaded that before very long you will discover that, as a place of residence for two lone, lorn young women, Clover Cottage has its drawbacks."

When Ella returned from saying farewell to Mr. Martyn in the hall, she glanced at Madge and laughed.

"Jack's in his prophetic mood."

"I shouldn't be surprised if his prophecy's inspired."

Her tone was unexpectedly serious. Ella stared.

"What do you mean?"

"What I say."

"You're oracular, my dear. What do you say?"

"That I think it quite possible that we shall find that residence at Clover Cottage has its drawbacks; I've lighted on one or two of them already."

Ella leaned against the edge of the table, regarding the speaker with twinkling eyes and smiling lips.

"My dear, you don't mean to say that that crazy creature has left such an impression on your mind?"

"You see, my dear Ella, I haven't told you all the story. I felt that I had given Mr. Martyn a sufficient handle against us as it was; so I refrained."

"Pray what else is there to tell? To judge from your looks and manner one would think that there was something dreadful."

"I don't know about dreadful, but there certainly is something—odd. To begin with, that wretched woman was not my only visitor."

Then the rest of the tale was told—and this time the whole of it. Ella heard of the stranger who had intruded on the pretence of seeking music lessons: of his fear of the seedy loafer in the street; of his undignified exit through the back door; and the whole of his singular behaviour.

"And you say he could play?"

"Play! He played like an—I was going to say an angel, but I'll substitute artist."

"And he looked like a gentleman?"

"Certainly, and spoke like one."

"But he didn't behave like one?"

"I won't go so far as to say that. He said or did nothing that was positively offensive when he was once inside the house."

"But you called him a thief?"

"Yes; but, mind you, I didn't think he was one. I felt so angry."

"I should think you did. I should have felt murderous. And you don't think the man in the road was a policeman?"

"Not he. He was as evil-looking a vagabond as ever I saw."

"It doesn't follow merely on that account, my dear, that he wasn't a policeman."

There was malice in the lady's tones.

"Not at all; but even a policeman of that type would hardly have jumped out of his skin with fright at the sight of that horrible woman. He knew her, and she knew him. There's a mystery somewhere."

"How nice!"

"Nice? You think so? I wish you had interviewed her instead of me. My dear Ella, she—she was—beyond expression."

Ella came and seated herself on a stool at Madge's feet. Leaning her arms on her knees she looked up at her face.

"Poor old chap! It wasn't an agreeable experience."

Madge's answer was as significant as it was curt.

"It wasn't."

She gave further details of what the woman had said and done, and of how she had said and done it—details which she had omitted, for reasons of her own, in Mr. Martyn's presence. By the time she had finished the listener was as serious as the narrator.

"It makes me feel creepy to hear you."

"It would have made you creepy to have heard her. I felt as if the house was peopled with ghosts."

"Madge, don't! You'll make me want to sleep with you if you go on like that. Poor old chap! I'm sorry if I seemed to chaff you." She reflected before she spoke again. "I can see that it can't be nice for you to be alone in the house while I'm away in town all day, earning my daily bread—especially now that the days are drawing in. If you like, we'll clear out of this, this week—we could do it at a pinch— and we'll return to the seething masses."

Madge reflected, in her turn, before she answered.

"Nothing of the sort has happened before, and nothing may happen again. But I tell you frankly, that, if my experiences of to-day do recur, it won't take much to persuade me that I have an inclination towards the society of my fellows, and that I prefer even the crushes of Petticoat Lane to the solitudes of Wandsworth Common."

"Well, in that case, it shall be Petticoat Lane."

There was silence. Presently Madge stretched herself—and yawned.

"In the meantime," suggested Ella, putting her hand up to her own lips, "what do you say to bed?" And it was bed. "Would you like me to sleep with you," inquired Ella as they went upstairs; "because if you would like me to very much, I would."

"No," said Madge, "I wouldn't. I never did like to share my bed with any one, and I never shall. I like to kick about, and I like to have plenty of room to do it in."

"Very good—have plenty of room to do it in. Ungrateful creature! If you're haunted, don't call to me for aid."

As it happened, Madge did call to her for aid, after a fashion; though it was not exactly because she was haunted.

CHAPTER IV

IN THE DEAD OF NIGHT

Madge was asleep almost as soon as she was between the sheets, and it seemed to her that as soon as she was asleep she was awake again—waking with that sudden shock of consciousness which is not the most agreeable way of being roused from slumber, since it causes us to realise too acutely the fact that we have been sleeping. Something had woke her; what, she could not tell. She lay motionless, listening with that peculiar intensity with which one is apt to listen when woke suddenly in the middle of the night. The room was dark. There was the sound of distant rumbling: they were at work upon the line, where they would sometimes continue shunting from dusk to dawn. She could hear, faintly, the crashing of trucks as they collided the one with the other. A breeze was murmuring across the common. It came from Clapham Junction way—which was how she came to hear the noise of the shunting. All else was still. She must have been mistaken. Nothing had roused her. She must have woke her own accord.

Stay!—what was that? Her keen set ears caught some scarcely uttered sound. Was it the creaking of a board? Well, boards will creak at night, when they have a trick of being as audible as if they were exploding guns. It came again—and again. It was unmistakably a board that creaked—downstairs. Why should a board creak like that downstairs, unless—it was being stepped upon? As Madge strained her hearing, she became convinced that there were footsteps down below—stealthy, muffled footsteps, which would have been inaudible had it not been for the tell-tale boards. Some one was creeping along the passage. Suddenly there was a noise as if a coin, or a key, or some small object, had fallen to the floor. Possibly it was something of the kind which had roused her. It was followed by silence—as if the person who had caused the noise was waiting to learn if it had been overheard. Then once more the footsteps—she heard the door of the sitting-room beneath her open, and shut, and knew that some one had entered the room.

In an instant she was out of bed. She hurried on a pair of bedroom slippers which she kept beside her on the floor, and an old dressing-gown which was handy on a chair, moving as quickly and as noiselessly as the darkness would permit. Snatching up her candlestick, with its box of matches, she passed, without a moment's hesitation, as noiselessly as possible from the room. On the landing without she stood, for a second or two, listening. There could be no doubt about it—some one was in the sitting-room. Someone who wished to make himself or herself as little conspicuous as possible; but whose presence was still sufficiently obvious to the keen-eared auditor.

Madge went to Ella's room, and, turning the handle, entered. As she did so, she could hear Ella start up in bed.

"Who's there?" she cried.

"Hush! It's I. There's some one in the sitting-room."

Lighting a match, Madge applied it to the candle. Ella was sitting up in bed, staring at her, with tumbled hair and sleepy eyes, apparently only half awake.

"Madge!—what do you mean?"

"What I say. We're about to experience another of the drawbacks of rural residence. There's some one in the sitting-room—another uninvited guest."

"Are you sure?"

"Quite. If you care to go downstairs and look, you'll be sure."

"Whatever shall we do?"

"Do!—I'll show you what we'll do. Where's that revolver of Jack Martyn's, which he lent you?"

"It's in my handkerchief drawer—but it's loaded."

"All the better. I've fired off a revolver before to-day, and I am quite willing, at a pinch, to fire off another one to-night. I'll show you what we'll do." While she spoke, Madge had been searching the drawer in question. Now she stood with the weapon in her hand. "Perhaps you'll be so good as to get out of bed, and put something on, unless you prefer to go downstairs as the Woman in White. I suppose you're not afraid?"

Ella had got so far out of bed as to sit on the side, with her feet dangling over the edge.

"Well—I don't know that I am exactly afraid, but if you ask me if being woke in the middle of the night, to be told there's burglars in the house, is the kind of thing I'm fond of, I'll admit it isn't."

Madge laughed. Ella's tone, and air of exceeding ruefulness, apparently struck her as comical.

"It occurs to me, Miss Duncan, that it won't be long before Mr. Martyn makes a convert of you. As for me, now my blood's getting up—and it is getting up—I am beginning to think that it is rather fun."

"Are you? Then I'm afraid your sense of humour must be keener than mine." She followed Madge's example—putting on a pair of slippers and a dressing-gown. "Now, what are you going to do?"

"I'm going down to ask our guest to show me his card of invitation."

"Madge! Hadn't we better open the window and scream? Or you might fire into the air—if you're sure you do know how to fire a revolver."

"I'll soon show you if I know—and I'll show our visitor too. And I don't think we'd better open the window and scream. Are you coming?"

Madge moved out of the room, Ella going after her with a rush.

"Madge!—don't leave me!"

The two girls stood listening at the top of the stairs—Madge with the candlestick in one hand, and the revolver in the other.

"It strikes me that we sha'n't be able to inquire for that card of invitation, because he doesn't mean to stay for us to ask him. His intention is not to stand upon the order of his going, but to go at once."

Apparently the proceedings in Ella's bedroom had been audible below. Evidently the person in the sitting-room had become startled. There was a stampede of heavy feet across the floor; the noise of furniture being hastily pushed aside; then they could hear the sound of the window being unlatched, and opened. It was plain that the intruder, whoever it was, was bent on showing a clean pair of heels.

It seemed as if the certitude of this fact had inspired Ella with sudden courage. Anyhow, she there and then shouted, with the full force of her lungs, as if she all at once had found her voice.

"Who's that downstairs?"

"Speak!" exclaimed Madge, with a nearly simultaneous yell, "or I fire!"

And she did fire—though no one spoke; or, for the matter of that, had a chance of speaking; for the words and the shot came both together. What she fired at was not quite plain, since, if appearances could be trusted, the bullet lodged in the ceiling; for, at the same moment, a small shower of plaster came tumbling down.

"Madge!" cried Ella. "I believe you've sent the bullet right through the roof! How you frightened me!"

"It was rather a startler," admitted Madge, in whose voice there seemed a slight tendency to tremor. "I'd no idea it would make such a noise—the other revolver I fired didn't. Ella!—what are you doing?"

The question was induced by the fact that Ella had rushed to the landing window, thrown the sash up, thrust her head out, and was shouting as loudly as she could:

"Thieves! thieves!—help!"

Madge came up and put her head out beside her.

"Can you see him? Has he gone?"

"Of course he's gone—there he is, running down the road."

"Are you sure it's a man?"

"A man! It's a villain!—Help! thieves! help!"

"Don't make that noise. What's the use? No one can hear you, and it only gives him the impression that we're afraid of him, which we're not; as, if he comes back again, we'll show him. There's more bullets in this revolver than one—I remember Jack saying so; and I'm not forced to send them all through the roof."

Ella drew her head inside. There was colour in her cheeks, and fire in her eyes. Now that the immediate danger seemed past her humour was a ferocious one.

"I wish you'd shot him."

Madge was calmer, though still sufficiently sanguinary.

"Well—I couldn't very well shoot him if I never caught a glimpse of him, could I? But we'll do better next time."

Ella clenched her fists, and her teeth too.

"Next time!—Oh, I think a burglar's the most despicable wretch on the face of the earth, and, if I had my way, I'd send every one caught in the act right straight to the gallows."

"Precisely—when caught. But you can scarcely effect a capture by standing on the top of the stairs, and inquiring of the burglar if he's there."

"I know I behaved like a coward—you needn't remind me. But that was because I was taken by surprise. If he were to come back—"

"Yes—if he were to come back?" Madge looked out of the window—casually. "I fancy there's some one coming down the road—it may be he returning."

Ella clutched at her arm.

"Madge!"

"You needn't be alarmed, my dear, I was mistaken; it's no one after all. Suppose, instead of breathing threatenings and slaughters 'after the battle is over,' we go down and see what mementoes of his presence our visitor has left behind—or, rather, what mementoes he has taken with him."

"Are you sure he was alone?"

"We shall be able to make sure by going down to see."

"Oh, Madge, do you think—"

"No, my dear, I don't, or I should be no more desirous of going down than you. I'm only willing to go and see if there is some one there because I'm sure there isn't."

There was not—luckily. There was little conspicuously heroic about the bearing of the young ladies as they descended the stairs to suggest that they would have made short work of any ruthless ruffian who might have been in hiding. About halfway down, Madge gave what was perhaps an involuntary little cough; at which Ella started as if the other had been guilty of a crime; and both paused as if fearful that something dreadful might ensue. The sitting-room door was closed. They hung about the handle as if it had been the entrance to some Bluebeard's den, and unimaginable horrors were concealed within. When Madge, giving the knob a courageous twist, flung the door wide open, Ella's face was pasty white. Both perceptibly retreated, as if expecting some monster to spring out on them. But no one sprang— apparently because there was no one there.

A current of cold air came from the room.

"The window's open."

Ella's voice was tremulous. Her tremor had the effect of making Madge sarcastic.

"That's probably because our visitor opened it. You could hardly expect him to stop to close it, could you?"

She went boldly into the room—Ella hard on her heels. She held the candle above her head—to have it almost blown out by the draught. She placed it on the table.

"If we want to have a light upon the subject, we shall have to shut that window."

She did so. Then looked about her.

"Well, he doesn't seem to have left many tokens of his presence. There's a chair knocked over, and he's pushed the cloth half off the table, but I don't see anything else."

"He seems to have taken nothing."

"Probably that was because there was nothing worth his taking. If he came here in search of plunder, he must have gone away a disgusted man."

"If he came here in search of plunder?—what else could he have come for?"

"Ah! that's the question."

"What's this?" Stooping, Ella picked up something off the floor. "Here's something he's left behind, at any rate."

She was holding a scrap of paper.

"What is it—a pièce de conviction of the first importance: the button off the coat by means of which the infallible detective hunts down the callous criminal?"

"I don't know what it is. It's a sort of hieroglyphic—if it isn't—nonsense."

Madge went and looked over her shoulder. Ella was holding half a sheet of dirty white notepaper, on which was written, with very bad ink and a very bad pen, in a very bad hand:—

"TOM OSSINGTON'S GHOST."

"Right—Straight across—three—four—up.

"Right—cat—dog—cat—dog—cat—dog—cat—dog—left eye—push."

The two girls read to the end—then over again. Then they looked at each other—Madge with smiling eyes.

"That's very instructive, isn't it?"

"Very. There seems to be a good deal of cat and dog about it."

"There does, I wonder what it means."

"If it means anything."

Madge, taking the paper from Ella's hand, went with it closer to the candle. She eyed it very shrewdly, turning it over and over, and making as if she were endeavouring to read between the lines.

"Do you know, Ella, that there is something curious about this."

"I suppose there is, since it's gibberish; and gibberish is curious."

"No, I'm not thinking of that. I'm thinking of the heading—'Tom Ossington's Ghost.' Do you know that that enterprising stranger, who came in search of music lessons he didn't want, asked me if my name was Ossington, and if no one of that name lived here."

"Are you sure Ossington was the name he mentioned? It's an unusual one."

"Certain; it was because it was an unusual one that I particularly noticed it. Then that dreadful woman was full of her ghosts, even claiming, as you heard, to be the ghost's wife. Doesn't it strike you, under the circumstances, as odd that the paper the burglar has left behind him, should be headed 'Tom Ossington's Ghost'?"

"It does seem queer—though I don't know what you are driving at."

"No; I don't know what I am driving at either. But I do know that I am driving at something. I'm beginning to think that I shall see a glimmer of light somewhere soon—though at present I haven't the faintest notion where."

"Do you think it was either of your visitors who has paid us another call to-night?"

"No; but I tell you what I do think."

"What?"

"I shouldn't be surprised if we've been favoured with a call from the individual who wasn't one of my visitors; the man in the road, who took to his heels in such a hurry at the sight of the woman."

"What cause have you to suppose that?"

"None whatever, I admit it frankly; but I do suppose it all the same. In the first place the man was burning to be one of my visitors, of that I'm persuaded—and he would have been if the woman hadn't come along. And in the second, he looked a burglar every inch of him. Ella, I'll tell you what!" She brought her hand on to the table with a crash which made Ella start, "There's a mystery about this house—you mark my words and see. It's haunted—in one sense, if it isn't in another."

Ella cast furtive glances over her shoulder, which were suggestive of anything but a mind at ease.

"You've a comfortable way of talking, upon my word."

Madge threw her arms out in front of her.

"There is a mystery about the house; it's one of these old, ramshackle sort of places in which there is that kind of thing—I'm sure of it. Aren't you conscious of a sense of mystery about the place, and don't you feel it's haunted?"

"Madge, if you don't stop talking like that, I'll leave the house this instant."

"The notion is not altogether an agreeable one, I'll allow; but facts are—"

"What's that?"

"What's what?"

Ella, clutching at Madge's arm, stared over her shoulder with a face white as a sheet.

"Did—didn't I hear s-something in the kitchen?"

"Something in the kitchen? If you did hear something in the kitchen, I'll shoot that something as dead as a door nail."

Madge caught up the revolver, which she had placed on the table.

"Madge, for goodness sake don't do anything rash!"

"I will do something rash—if you call it rash to shoot at sight any scoundrel who ventures to intrude on my premises at this hour of the night!—and I'll do it quickly! Do you think I'm going to be played the fool with because I'm only a woman! I'll soon prove to you I'm not—that is, if it is to be proved by a little revolver practice."

Madge spoke at the top of her voice, her words seeming to ring through the house with singular clearness. But whether this was done for the sake of encouraging herself and Ella, or with the view of frightening a possible foe, was an open question. She strode out of the room with an air of surprising resolution. Ella clinging to her skirts and following her, simply because she dare not be left behind. As it chanced, the kitchen door was open. Madge marched bravely into the room—only to find that her display of courage was thrown away, since the room was empty.

Having made sure of this, Madge turned to Ella with a smile on her face—though her cheeks, like her friend's, were whiter than they were wont to be.

"You see, we are experiencing some of the disadvantages of two lone, lorn young women being the solitary inhabitants of a rural residence—Jack Martyn scores."

For answer Ella burst into tears. Madge took her in her arms—as well as she could, for the candle in one hand and the revolver in the other.

"Don't cry, girl; there's nothing to cry at. You'll laugh at and be ashamed of yourself in the morning. I'll tell you what—I'll make an exception!—you shall have half my bed, and for the rest of the night we'll sleep together."

CHAPTER V

The next morning, information was given to a passing policeman of the events of the night, and in the course of the day an officer came round from the local station to learn particulars. Madge received him in solitary state; she had refused Ella's offer to stop away from business to keep her company, declaring that for that day, at any rate, she would be safe from undesirable intruders.

The officer was a plain-clothes man, middle-aged, imperfectly educated, with the stolid, matter-of-fact, rather stupid-looking countenance which one is apt to find an attribute of the detective of fact, rather than fiction.

"You say you didn't see him?"

"I saw the back of him."

"Hum!" This stands for a sort of a kind of a sniff.

"Would you know him if you saw him again?"

"From the glimpse which I caught of him last night I certainly shouldn't. It was pretty dark, and he was twenty or thirty yards down the road when I first caught sight of his back."

"You didn't follow him?"

"We did not."

Madge smiled as she thought of how such a suggestion would have been received had it been made at the time.

"He came in through the back window and left through the front?"

"That's it."

"And he took nothing?"

"No—but he left something behind him—he left this."

Madge produced the half-sheet of paper which Ella had picked up from the floor.

"You're sure this was his property?"

"I'm sure it isn't ours, and I'm sure we found it in this room just after he left it."

The officer took the paper; read it, turned it over and over; looked it up and down; read it again. Then he gave his mouth a rather comical twist; then he looked at Madge with eyes which he probably intended to be pregnant with meaning.

"Hum!" He paused to cogitate. "I suppose you know there's been a burglary here before?"

"I know nothing of the kind. We have only been here six weeks, and are quite strangers to the place."

"There was. Something more than a year ago. The house was empty at the time. The man who did it was caught at the job—and our chap got pretty well knocked about for his pains. But that wasn't the only time we've had business at this house; our fellows have been here a good many times."

"Neither my friend or I had the slightest notion that the house had such a reputation."

"I daresay not. It's been empty a good long time. I expect the stories which were told about it were against its letting."

"What sort of stories?"

"All sorts—nonsense, most of them."

"Were the people who lived here named Ossington?"

"Ossington?" The officer screwed his mouth up into the comical twist which it seemed he had a trick of giving it. "I believe it was, or, at any rate, something like it. A queer lot they were—very."

"Do you see what's written as a heading on that piece of paper?"

The officer's glance returned to the writing.

"'Tom Ossington's Ghost!'—yes, I noticed it, but I don't know what it means—do you?"

"Except that if the name of the people who lived here last was Ossington, it would seem as if last night's affair had some reference to the house's former occupants."

"Yes—it would look as if it had—when you come to look at it in that way." He was studying it as if now he had made up his mind to understand it clearly. "It looks as if it was some sort of cryptogram, and yet it mightn't be—it's hard to tell." He wagged his head. "I'll take it to our chaps, and see what they can make of it. Some men are better at this sort of thing than others." Folding up the paper he placed it in his pocket-book. "Am I to understand that you can give no description of the burglar—that there's no one you suspect?"

"I don't know that it amounts to suspicion—but there was a man hanging about here in rather a singular fashion whom I can't help thinking might have had a finger in the pie."

"Can you describe him?"

"He was about my height—I'm five feet six and a half—thick set, and I noticed he walked in a sort of rolling way; I thought he was drunk at first, but I don't believe he was. He kept his hands in his trousers pockets, and he was very shabbily dressed, in an old black coat—I believe you call them Chesterfields—which was buttoned down the front right up to the chin—I doubt if he had a waistcoat; a pair of old patched trousers—and I'm under the impression that his boots were odd ones. He had an old black billycock hat, with no band on, crammed over his eyes, iron-grey hair, and a fortnight's growth of whiskers on his cheeks and chin. He had a half impudent, half hang-dog air—altogether just the sort of person to try his hand at this sort of thing."

"I'll take down that description, if you'll repeat it."

She did repeat it—and he did take it down, with irritating slowness. When she had finished he read what he had written, tapping his teeth with the end of his pencil and looking most important.

"I shouldn't be surprised if you've laid your finger on the very man—and if we lay our fingers on him before the day is over. You will excuse my saying, miss, that you've got the faculty of observation—marked. I couldn't have given a better description of a chap myself—and I've been a bit longer at the game than you have. Now I'll just go through the place once more, and then I'll go; and then in due course you'll hear from us again."

He did go through the place once more—and he did go.

"Now," observed Madge to herself, as she watched him going down the road, "all that remains, is for us in due course to hear from you again—to some effect—and that, if you're the sort of blunderbuss I take you to be, will be never."

Turning from the window, she looked about the room, speaking half in jest and half in earnest.

"This is a delightful state of things—truly! It seems as if we couldn't have found a more undesirable habitation, if we had tried Petticoat Lane. Not the first burglar that's been in the place! And the house well known to the police—not to speak of a sinister reputation in all the country side! Charming! Clover Cottage seems to be an ideal place of residence for two lone, lorn young women. The abode of mystery, and, so far as I can make out, a sink of crime, one wonders if it still waits to become the scene of some ghastly murder to give to the situation its crowning touches. I shiver—or, at any rate, I ought to shiver—when I reflect on the horrors with which I may be, and probably am, surrounded!"

Ella returned earlier than the day before, and, this time, she came alone. The question burst from her lips the instant she was in the house.

"Well, has anything happened?"

"Nothing—of importance. It's true the police have been, but as it appears that they've been here over and over again before, that's a trifle. There's been at least one previous burglar upon the premises, and it seems that the house has been known to the police—and to the whole neighbourhood—for years, in the most disreputable possible sense."

Ella could but gasp.

"Madge!"

The statements which the officer had made were retailed, with comments and additions—and, it may be added, interpolations. Ella was more impressed even than Madge had been—being divided between concern and indignation.

"To think that we should have been inveigled into taking such a place! We ought to claim damages from those scamps of agents who let it us without a word of warning. You can't think how I have been worrying about you the whole day long; the idea of our being together in the place is bad enough, but the idea of your being alone in it is worse. What that policeman has said, settles it. Jack may laugh if he likes, but my mind is made up that I won't stop a moment longer in the house than I can help; the notion of your being all those hours alone here would worry me into the grave if nothing else did—and so I shall tell him when he comes."

Madge's manner was more equable.

"He will laugh at you, you'll find; and, unless I'm in error, here he is to do it."

As she spoke there was a vigorous knock at the front door.

CHAPTER VI

THE LONG ARM OF COINCIDENCE

"Go," said Ella, as she hastened from the room, "and open the door, while I go upstairs and take my hat off."

Madge did as she was told. There were two persons at the door—Jack Martyn and another.

"This," said Jack, referring to his companion, "is a friend of mine."

It was dark in the passage, and Madge was a little flurried. She perceived that Jack had a companion, and that was all.

"Go into the sitting-room, I'll bring you a lamp in a minute. Ella has gone to take her hat off. '

Presently, returning with the lighted lamp in her hand, placing it on the table, she glanced at Jack's companion—and stared. In her astonishment, she all but knocked the lamp over. Jack laughed.

"I believe," he said, "you two have met before."

Madge continued speechless. She passed her hand before her eyes, as if to make sure she was not dreaming. Jack laughed again.

"I repeat that I believe you two have met before."

Madge drew herself up to her straightest and her stiffest. Her tone was icy.

"Yes, I rather believe we have."

She rather believed they had?—If she could credit the evidence of her own eyes the man in front of her was the stranger who had so unwarrantably intruded on pretence of seeking music lessons—who had behaved in so extraordinary a fashion!

"This," went on Jack airily, "is a friend of mine, Bruce Graham,—Graham, this is Miss Brodie."

Madge acknowledged the introduction with an inclination of the head which was so faint as to be almost imperceptible. Mr. Graham, on the contrary, bent almost double—he seemed scarcely more at his ease than she was.

"I'm afraid, Miss Brodie, that I've behaved very badly. I trust you will allow me to express my contrition."

"I beg you will not mention it," she turned away; "I will go and tell Ella you have come."

There came a voice from behind her.

"You needn't—Ella is aware of it already."

As Ella came into the room, she moved to leave it. Jack caught her by the arm.

"Madge, don't go away in a fume!—you wait till you have heard what I have got to say. Do you know that we're standing in the presence of a romance in real life—on the verge of a blood-curdling mystery? Fact!—aren't we, Graham?"

Mr. Graham's language was slightly less emphatic.

"We are, or rather we may be confronted by rather a curious condition of affairs."

Jack waved his arm excitedly.

"I say it's the most extraordinary thing. Now, honestly, Graham, isn't it a most extraordinary thing?"

"It certainly is rather a striking illustration of the long arm of coincidence."

"Listen to him. Isn't he cold-blooded? If you'd heard him an hour or two ago, he was hot enough to melt all the ice-cream in town. But you wait a bit. This is my show, and I'll let you know it. Sit down, Ella—sit down, Madge—Graham, take a chair. To you a tale I will unfold."

Taking up his position on the hearthrug in front of the fireplace, he commenced to orate.

"You see this man. His name's Graham. He digs in the same house I do. To be perfectly frank, his rooms are on the opposite side of the landing. You may have heard me speak of him."

"I have. Often!" This was Ella.

"Have you? You must know, Graham, that there are frequently occasions on which I have nothing whatever to talk about, so I fill up the blanks with what I may call padding. I say this, because I don't want you to misunderstand the situation. This morning he lunched at the same crib I did. Directly he came in I saw that he was below par; so I said—I always am a sympathetic soul—'I do hope, Graham, you won't forget to let me have an invitation to your funeral—and, in the meantime, perhaps you'll let me know of what it is you're dying?' Now, he's not one of those men who wear their hearts upon their sleeves for daws to peck at—you know the quotation, and if you don't, I do; and it was some time before I could extract a word from him, even edgeways. But at last he put down his knife and fork with a clatter—it was distinctly with a clatter—and he observed, 'Martyn, I've been misbehaving myself.' I was not surprised, and I told him so. 'I'm in a deuce of a state of mind because I've been insulting a lady.' 'That's nothing!' I replied. 'I'm always insulting a lady.'—I may explain that when I made that remark, Ella, you were the lady I had in my mind's eye. At this point I would pause to inquire why, Miss Brodie, you did not take me into your confidence yesterday afternoon?"

"I did."

"You did not."

"I did."

"You told me about the lunatic lady, because, I suppose, you could not help it—since you were caught in the act—but you said nothing about a lunatic gentleman." He wagged his finger portentously. "Don't think you deceive me, Madge Brodie—I smell a rat, and one of considerable size."

"Jack, do go on."

This was Ella.

"I will go on—in my own way. If you bustle me, I'll keep going on for ever. Don't I tell you this is my show? Do you want to queer it? Well, as I was about to observe—when I was interrupted—Graham started spinning a yarn about how he had forced his way into a house, in which there was a young woman all alone, by herself, and, so far as I could make out, gone on awful. 'May I ask,' I said, beginning to think that his yarn smelt somewhat fishy, 'what house this was?' 'The place,' he replied, as cool as a cucumber, 'is called Clover Cottage.' 'What's that!' I cried—I almost jumped out of my chair. 'I say that the place is called Clover Cottage.' I had to hold on to the hair of my head with both my hands. 'And whereabouts may Clover Cottage be?' 'On Wandsworth Common.' When he said that, as calmly as if he were asking me to pass the salt, I collapsed. I daresay he thought that I'd gone mad."

"I began to wonder." This was Graham.

"Did you? Let me tell you, sir, that as far as you were concerned, I had long since passed the stage of wonder, and had reached the haven of assurance. 'Are you aware?' I cried, 'that Clover Cottage, Wandsworth Common, is the residence of the lady whom I hope to make my wife?' 'Good Lord!' he said. 'No,' I screamed, 'good lady!' I fancy the waiter, from his demeanour, was under the impression that I was about to fight; in which case I should have proved myself mad, because, as you perceive for yourselves, the man's a monster. 'It seems to me,' I said, 'that if the lady you insulted was not the lady whom I hope to make my wife, it was that lady's friend, which is the same thing—'"

"Is it?" interposed Ella. "You hear him, Madge?"

"I hear."

"'Which is the same thing,'" continued Jack. "'And therefore, sir, I must ask you to explain.' He explained, I am bound to admit that he explained there and then. He gave me an explanation which I have no hesitation in asserting"—Jack, holding his left hand out in front of him, brought his right fist solemnly down upon his open palm—"was the most astonishing I ever heard. It shows the hand of Providence; it shows that the age of miracles is not yet past; it shows—"

Ella cut the orator short.

"Never mind what it shows; what's the explanation?"

Jack shook his head sadly.

"I was about to point out several other things which that explanation shows, with a view, as I might phrase it, of improving the occasion, but, having been interrupted for the third time, I refrain. The explanation itself you will hear from Graham's own lips—after tea. He is here for the purpose of giving you that explanation—after tea. I believe, Graham, I am correct in saying so?"

"Perfectly. Only, so far as I am concerned, I am ready to give my explanation now. I cannot but feel that I shall occupy an invidious position in, at any rate, Miss Brodie's eyes until I have explained."

"Then feel! I'll be hanged if you shall explain now. Dash it, man, I want my tea; I want a high tea, a good tea—at once!"

Ella sprang up from her chair.

"Come, Madge, let's give the man his tea."

It was a curious meal—if only because of the curious terms on which two members of the party stood toward each other. The two girls sat at each end of the table, the men on either side. Madge, unlike her usual self, was reserved and frosty; what little she did say was addressed to Ella or to Jack. Mr. Graham she ignored, treating his timorous attempts in a conversational direction with complete inattention. His position could hardly have been more uncomfortable. Ella, influenced by Madge's attitude, seemed as if she could not make up her mind how to treat him on her own account; her bearing towards him, to say the least, was chilly. On the other hand. Jack's somewhat cumbrous attempts at humour and sociability did not mend matters; and more than once before the meal was over Mr. Graham must have heartily wished that he had never sat down to it.

Still, even Madge might have admitted, and perhaps in her heart she did admit, that, under the circumstances, he bore himself surprisingly well; that he looked as if he was deserving of better treatment. Half unconsciously to herself—and probably quite unconsciously to him—she kept a corner of her eye upon him all the time. He scarcely looked the sort of man to do anything unworthy. The strong rough face suggested honesty, the bright clear eyes were frank and open; the broad brow spelt intellect, the lines of the mouth and jaw were bold and firm. The man's whole person was suggestive of strength, both physical and mental. And when he came to tell the story which Jack Martyn had foreshadowed, it was difficult, as one listened, not to believe that he was one who had been raised by nature above the common sort. He told his tale with a dramatic earnestness, and yet a simple, modest sincerity, which held his hearers from the first, and which, before he had done, had gained them all over to his side.

CHAPTER VII

BRUCE GRAHAM'S FIRST CLIENT

"I don't know," he began, "if Martyn has told you that by profession I am a barrister."

"No," said Jack, as he shook his head, "I have told them nothing to your credit."

Graham smiled; the smile lighting up his features, and correcting what was apt to be their chief defect, a prevailing sombreness.

"I am a barrister—one of the briefless brigade. One morning, about fourteen months ago, I left London for a spin on my bicycle. It was the long vacation; every one was out of town except myself. I thought I would steal a day with the rest. I came through Wandsworth, meaning to go across Wimbledon Common, through Epsom, and on towards the Shirley Hills. As I came down St. John's Hill my tyre caught up a piece of broken glass off the road, and the result was a puncture, or rather a clean cut, nearly an inch in length. I took it to a repairing shop by the bridge. As I stood waiting for the job to be done, two policemen came along with a man handcuffed between them, a small crowd at their heels.

"I asked the fellow who was doing my cycle what was wrong. He told me that there had been a burglary at a house on the Common the night before, that the burglar had been caught in the act, had half-murdered the policeman who had caught him, and was now on his way to the magistrate's court.

"As it seemed likely that the mending of my tyre would take some time, actuated by a more or less professional curiosity, I followed the crowd to the court.

"The case was taken up without delay. The statement that the constable who had detected what was taking place had been half-murdered was an exaggeration, as the appearance of the officer himself in the witness-box disclosed. But he had been roughly handled. His head was bandaged, he carried his arm in a sling, and he bore himself generally as one who had been in the wars. My experience, small as it is, teaches that constables on such occasions are wont, perhaps not unnaturally, to make the most of their injuries; and, to say the least, the prisoner had not escaped scot free. His skull had been laid open, two of his teeth had been knocked down his throat, his whole body was black and blue with bruises. Indeed his battered appearance so excited my sympathy that then and there I offered him my gratuitous services in his defence. My offer was accepted. I did what I could.

"However, there was very little that could be done. The burglary, it seemed, had occurred at a place called Clover Cottage."

"Why," cried Ella, "this is Clover Cottage!"

"Yes," said Jack, shaking his head with what he meant to be mysterious significance, "as you correctly observe, this is Clover Cottage. Didn't I tell you you'd see the hand of Providence? You just wait a bit, you'll be dumbfounded."

Mr. Graham continued.

"Clover Cottage it appeared was unoccupied. There were in it neither tenants nor goods. So far as the evidence showed, it contained nothing at all. Being found in an absolutely empty house is not, as a rule, an offence which meets with a severe punishment. I was at a loss, therefore, to understand why my client should have made such a desperate defence and thus have enormously increased the measure of his guilt in the way he had done. Had it not been for what was termed, and perhaps rightly, his assault on the police, the affair would have been settled out of hand. As it was, the magistrate felt that he had no option but to send the case to trial; which he did do there and then.

"Before his trial I had more than one interview with my client in his cell at Wandsworth Gaol. He told me, by way of explaining his conduct, an extraordinary story; so extraordinary that, from that hour to this, I have never been able to make up my mind as to its truth.

"Under ordinary circumstances I should have had no hesitation in affirming his statement, or rather his series of statements, was a more or less badly contrived set of lies. But there was something about the fellow which assured me that at any rate he himself believed what he said. He was by no means an ordinary criminal type, and there seemed no reason to doubt his assertion that this was the first felonious transaction he had ever had a hand in. He admitted he had led an irregular life, and that he had come down the ladder of respectability with a run, but he stoutly maintained that this was the first time he had ever done anything deserving the attention of the police.

"He was a man about forty years of age; he claimed to be only thirty-six. If that was the fact, then the life he had been living, and the injuries he had recently received, made him look considerably older. His name, he said, was Charles Ballingall. By trade he was a public-house broker; once, and that not so long ago, in a very fair way of business. He had had a lifelong friend—I am telling you the story, you understand, exactly as he told it me—named Ossington—Thomas Ossington. Ballingall always spoke of him as Tom Ossington."

Ellen looked at Madge.

"Madge!" she exclaimed, "how about Tom Ossington's Ghost?"

"I know."

Madge sat listening with compressed lips and flashing eyes; that was all she vouchsafed to reply. Mr. Graham glanced in her direction as he went on.

"According to Ballingall's story, Ossington must have been a man of some eccentricity. He was possessed of considerable means—according to Ballingall, of large fortune. But his whole existence had been embittered by the fact that he suffered from some physical malformation. For one thing, he had a lame foot—"

"I know that he was lame." This was Madge; all eyes stared at her.

"You knew? How did you know?"

"Because she told me."

Ella's eyes opened wider.

"She told you? Who?"

"The ghost's wife."

"The ghost's wife!"

"Yes, the ghost's wife. But never mind about that now. Mr. Graham will perhaps go on."

And Mr. Graham went on.

"This had preyed upon his spirits his whole life long; and, as his unwillingness to show himself among his fellows increased, it had made of him almost a recluse. He was, however, as it seemed, a man of strong affections, tender heart, and simple disposition. In these respects Ballingall could not speak of him with sufficient warmth. There never had been, he declared, a man like Tom. There was nothing he would not do for a friend—self-abnegation was the passion of his life. Ballingall owned that he owed everything to Ossington. Ossington had set him up in business, had helped him in a hundred ways. In return he (Ballingall) had rewarded him with the most hideous ingratitude. This part of the story was accompanied by such a strong exhibition of remorse that I, for one, found it difficult not to believe in the fellow's genuineness.

"In spite of his mis-shapenness, Ossington had found a wife, apparently a lovely one. The man loved her with the single-eyed affection of which such natures as his are capable. She, on the other hand, was as unworthy of his affection as she possibly could have been. From Ballingall's account she was evil through and through; he could find no epithet too evil to hurl at her. But then it was very possible that he was prejudiced. According to him, this woman, Ossington's wife, loathing her devoted husband, full to the lips with scorn of him, had deliberately laid herself out to win his (Ballingall's) love, and had succeeded so completely as to have caused him to forget the mountain-load of gratitude under which he ought to have stumbled, even to the extent of causing him to steal his friend's wife—the wife who was the very light of that friend's eyes.

"I think there was some truth in the fellow's version of the crime—for crime it was, and of the blackest dye. He declared to me that as soon as the thing was done, he knew himself to be the ineffable hound which he indeed was. The veil which the woman's allurements and sophistries had spread before his eyes was torn into shreds, and he saw the situation in all its horrible reality. She was as false to him as she had been to her husband, and he had been to his friend. In a few months she had left him, having ruined him before she went. From that time his career was all downhill. Remorse pursued him day and night. He felt that he was a pariah—an outcast among men; that an ineffaceable brand was on his brow which would for ever stamp him as accursed. It is possible that under the stress of privation,—for he quickly began to suffer actual privation—his mind became unhinged. But that he had suffered, and was still suffering, acutely, for his crime, the sweat of agony which broke out upon his brow as he told his tale was, to me, sufficient evidence.

"Two or three years passed. He sank to about the lowest depths to which a man could sink. At last, ragged, penniless, hungry, he was refused a job as a sandwich-man because of his incapacity to keep up with his fellows. One night he was on the Surrey side of the Embankment, near Westminster Bridge. It was after one o'clock in the morning; shortly before, he had heard Big Ben striking the hour. He was leaning over the parapet in front of Doulton's factory—you will observe that I reproduce the attention to detail which characterised this portion of his story, such an impression did it make upon my mind. As he stood looking at the water, some one touched him on the shoulder. Supposing it was a policeman who suspected his intentions, he turned hastily round. To his astonishment it was Tom Ossington. 'Tom!' he gasped.

"'Charlie!' returned the other. 'Come the first thing to-morrow morning to Clover Cottage.'

"Without another word he walked rapidly away in the direction of the Wandsworth Road—Ballingall distinctly noticing, as he went, that his limp had perceptibly diminished. Left once more alone, Ballingall was at a loss what to make of the occurrence. Ossington's appearance at that particular moment, so far away from home at that hour of the night, was a problem which he found it difficult to solve. He at last decided that the man's incurable tender-heartedness had caused him to at least partially overlook the blackness of the offence, and to offer his whilom friend succour in the depths of his distress. Anyhow, the next morning found the broken-down wretch in front of Ossington's house—of this house, as I understand."

As Mr. Graham said this, for some reason or other at least two of its hearers shivered; Ella clasped her hands more tightly as they lay upon her knee, and the expression of Madge's wide-open eyes grew more intense. Even Jack Martyn seemed subdued.

"To his indescribable astonishment, the house was empty. A board in the garden announced that it was to be let or sold. As he stood staring, a policeman came along.

"'Excuse me!' he said, 'but doesn't Mr. Ossington live here?'

"'He did!' answered the policeman; 'but he doesn't now.'

"'Can you tell me where he is living? I want to know because he asked me to call on him.'

"'Did he? Then if he asked you to call on him, I should if I was you. You'll find him in Wandsworth Churchyard. That's where he is living now!'

"The policeman's tone was jocular, Ballingall's appearance was against him. Evidently the officer suspected him of some clumsy attempt at invention. But as soon as the words were uttered Ballingall staggered back against the wall, according to his own account, like one stricken with death. He was speechless. The policeman, with a laugh, turned on his heel and left him there. Impelled by some influence which he could not resist, the conscience-haunted vagabond dragged his wearied feet to the churchyard. There among the tombstones he found one which purported to be erected to the memory of Thomas Ossington, who had been interred there some two years previously. While he stared, thunderstruck, at the inscription, Ballingall assured me that Tom Ossington stood at his side, and pointed at it with his finger."

Graham paused. His listeners fidgeted in their seats. It was a second or two before the narrator continued.

"You understand that I am telling you the story precisely as it was told me, without accepting for it any responsibility whatever. I can only assure you that whilst it was being told, I was so completely held, by what I can best describe as the teller's frenzied earnestness, that I accepted his facts precisely as he told them, and it was only after I got away from the glamour of his intensity of self-conviction that I perceived how entirely irreconcilable they were with the teachings of our everyday experience.

"Thenceforward, Ballingall declared that he was never without a feeling that Ossington was somewhere in the intermediate neighbourhood—to use his own word, that he was shadowing him. For the next week or two he lighted upon somewhat better times. He obtained a job at road-cleaning, and in one way or another managed to preserve himself from actual starvation. But, shortly, the luck ran out, and one night he again found himself without a penny with which to buy either food or lodging. He was struggling up Southampton Street, in the Strand, intending to hang about the purlieus of Covent Garden with the faint hope that he might be able to get some sort of job at the dawn of day, when he saw, coming towards him from the market, Tom Ossington. Ballingall shrank back into the doorway, and, while he stood there shivering, Ossington came and planted himself in front of him.

"'Charlie!' he said, 'why didn't you come to Clover Cottage when I told you?'

"Ballingall protested that he looked and spoke just like a rational being—with the little air of impatience which had always been his characteristic; that there was nothing either in his manner or his appearance in any way unusual, and that there was certainly nothing to suggest an apparition. A conversation was carried on between them just as it might have been between an ordinary Jones and Robinson.

"'I did come!' he replied.

"'Yes—but you stopped outside. Why didn't you come inside?'

"'Because the house was empty!'

"'That's all you know.'

"'Yes,' repeated Ballingall, 'that's all I do know.'

"'There's my fortune in that house!'

"'Your fortune?'

"'Yes my fortune; all of it. I brought it home, and hid it away—after Lily went.'

"Lily was his wife's name. He spoke of her with a sort of gasp. Ballingall felt as if he had been struck.

"'What's your fortune to do with me?'

"'Everything maybe—because it is yours, if you'll come and get it; every farthing. It's anyone's who finds it, anyone's—I don't care who it is. What does it matter to me who has it—now? Why shouldn't it be yours? There's heaps and heaps of money, heaps! More than you suppose. It'll make a rich man of you—set you up for life, buy you houses, carriages and all. You have only got to come and get it, and it is yours. Think of what a difference it'll make to you—of all that it will do for you—of all that it will mean. It will pick you out of the gutter, and place you in a mansion, with as many servants as you like to pay for at your beck and call. And all yours for the fetching—or anyone's for the matter of that. But why shouldn't you make it yours? Don't be a fool, but come, man, come!'

"He continued urging and entreating Ballingall to come and take for his own the treasures which he declared were hidden away in Clover Cottage, until, turning round, without a farewell word, he walked down the street and disappeared into the Strand.

"Ballingall assured me that he didn't know what to make of it; and if he was speaking the truth, I quite understand his difficulty. He was aware that, neither physically nor mentally, was he in the best of health, and he knew also that Ossington was continually in his mind. He might be the victim of hallucination; but if so, it was hallucination of an extraordinary sort. He himself had not touched Ossington, but Ossington had touched him. His touch had been solid enough, he looked solid enough, but how came he to be in Southampton Street if he was lying in Wandsworth Churchyard? On the other hand, the story of the hidden fortune was quite in accordance with what he knew of the man's character. He always had a trick of concealing money, valuables, all sorts of things, in unusual places. And for him to have secreted the bulk of his capital, or even the whole of it, or what represented the whole of it, and then to have left the hiding-place unrevealed, for some one to discover after he was dead and gone, was just the sort of thing he might have been expected to do.

"Anyhow, Ballingall did not go to Clover Cottage the following day. He found a job when the market opened, and that probably had a good deal to do with his staying away. The next night Ossington returned—if I remember rightly, just as Ballingall was about to enter a common lodging-house. And he came back not that night only, but over and over again, so far as I could understand, for weeks together, and always with the same urgent request, that he would come and fetch the fortune which lay hidden in Clover Cottage.

"At last torn by conflicting doubts, driven more than half insane—as he himself admitted—by the feeling that his life was haunted, he did as his mysterious visitor desired—he went to Clover Cottage. He hung about the house for an hour. At last, persuaded that it was empty, he gained admission through the kitchen window. No sooner was he in than a constable who, unconsciously to himself, had been observing his movements with suspicious eyes, came and found him on the premises. The feeling that, after all, he had allowed himself to be caught in something that looked very like a trap, bereft Ballingall of his few remaining senses, and he resisted the officer with a degree of violence which he would not have shown had he retained his presence of mind.

"The result was that instead of leaving Clover Cottage the possessor of a fortune, he left it to be hauled ignominiously to the stationhouse."

CHAPTER VIII

"And is that all the story?" asked Ella, for Mr. Graham had paused.

"All of it as it relates to Ballingall. So far as he was concerned, it brought his history up to date."

"And what became of him?"

"He was tried at the Surrey Sessions. There was practically no defence—for, of course, I could not urge on his behalf the wild story he had told me. All I could do was to plead extenuating circumstances. He was found guilty, and got twelve months."

"And then?"

"Then I came in—that was my first brief, and my last. Although I could not see my way to shape his story into the form of any legal plea, still less could I erase it from my mind. Never had I heard such a tale before, and never had I listened to a man who had so impressed me by his complete sincerity as Ballingall had done when telling it. He had struck me as being as sane as I myself was; had used commonplace words; had not gone out of his way to heighten their colour; but had simply told the thing straight on, exactly as it occurred. I felt convinced that, from his own point of view, the affair was genuine.

"Months went by, and still the story stuck in my brain. I found myself putting propositions of this kind. There was a house called Clover Cottage, and there had lived in it a man named Ossington, an avowed eccentric—for I had made inquiries in the neighbourhood, and had learned that he had been regarded thereabouts as more or less insane. Suppose, in this empty house of his, he had hidden something which was more or less valuable, for which there existed no actual owner, nor any designated heir. What then?"

The speaker paused again. Then spoke more softly. On his countenance the shadows seemed to deepen.

"You must understand that I am a poor man. All the world that knows me is conscious of my poverty, but none but myself is aware how poor I really am. I have felt, and feel, that if I can only hold on, I shall win my way in my profession yet. But it is the holding on which is so difficult. Some time ago I came to the end of my resources, and during the last year I have been living from hand to mouth. Had I had my time more fully occupied I should have been able to banish from my mind the man's queer story; or had I seen my way to earn money sufficient to supply my daily needs, anyhow, without forfeiting my right to call myself a professional man, and so barring that gate to my future advancement; my thoughts would not have turned so frequently to that possibly hidden, useless hoard. I was frequently conscious that the whole thing might be, and probably was, a pure phantasm, and that there was no such hoard, and never had been; but, at the same time I was persuaded that Ballingall had not been a conscious liar.

"Things came to such a pitch that I found myself in possession of less than ten shillings, and with nothing pawnable on which to raise the wind—you must forgive my entering on these details, but it is absolutely necessary if you are to have a complete comprehension of my position. This, I told myself, was absurd, and if there really was something hidden at Clover Cottage worth having, which could be had for the finding, it was absurder still. I started then and there with a half-formed resolution to put the matter to a final test, and to look for myself. I reached Clover Cottage—to find that it was occupied. There was a plate outside, announcing that lessons were given in music. My mind had been in a tolerable state of confusion when I started. I was conscious of the apparent absurdity of my quest; and that consciousness had not grown less as I went on. The discovery that the house was tenanted made my confusion worse confounded. More than half ashamed of my errand, I was wholly at a loss what to do. While I hesitated, I chanced to glance up, and there, a few yards down the road, was ... Ballingall."

"I knew it was Ballingall."

This was Madge.

Ella turned on her.

"You knew it was Ballingall?—How did you know it was Ballingall? It seems to me that you know everything."

"Miss Brodie," observed Bruce Graham, "very naturally draws her own conclusions. The sight of him turned me into a drivelling idiot. In the confusion of my mind his appearance on the scene at that particular moment seemed nothing short of supernatural. I felt as if I had been guilty of some act of treachery towards him, and as if he had sprung from goodness alone knew where to catch me in the very act. I blundered through the gate, knocked at the door and almost forced my way into the house."

"You did almost force your way into the house."

Madge's tone was grim.

"I'm afraid I did—and, being in, I blurted out some nonsense about being in search of music lessons, and generally misbehaved myself all round. As a climax, just as I was about to put an end to my intrusion, I saw Ballingall staring at me through the window. I would not have encountered him then for all the hidden hoards the world contains. I entreated Miss Brodie—to permit me to make my escape through the back door—and she did."

"Yes, and insulted you as you went."

Graham rose from his seat.

"You behaved to me, Miss Brodie, infinitely better than I deserved. You would have been perfectly justified in summoning a policeman, and giving me into charge. I can only thank you for your forbearance. I assure you of my most extreme penitence. And while I cannot expect that you will forgive me at once—"

"But I do forgive you."

Madge had also risen.

"Miss Brodie."

"Of course I do. And I did behave badly—like a wretch. But why didn't you explain?"

"You saw what, at the moment, was my capacity to explain, and now you perceive how extremely complicated the explanation would have had to be."

"But to think," cried Ella, "that we should be in the very centre of a mystery."

Jack struck in.

"Exactly—living in the very heart of it; surrounded by it on every side; having it staring you in the face whichever way you turn. What did I tell you? Isn't it blood-curdling? Like the man says in the song—you really never do know where you are."

Ella glanced at Madge.

"The burglary last night—do you think?"

"Of course it was."

"Ballingall?"

"Without a doubt."

"But, my dear, how can you be so sure?"

"He was hanging about all day—he tried again last night; it's as plain as it possibly can be."

Jack, puzzled, had been looking from one to the other.

"Perhaps you will tell us what is as plain as it possibly can be."

Ella turned to him.

"There was another burglary last night."

"Where?"

"Here—in the very middle of the night."

"Upon my honour!—this appears to be—Graham, this really does appear to be a pleasant house to live in. The delights of the country, with the horrors of town thrown in.—Did you catch the ruffian?"

"Madge heard him first."

"Oh—Madge heard him first?"

"Yes, and then she came and told me—"

"Where was he all the time?"

"Wait a bit, and I'll tell you. Then we both of us heard him—then Madge fired—"

"Fired?—what?"

"Your revolver."

"Gracious!—did she hit him?"

"She never saw him."

"Never saw him! Then what did she fire at?"

"Well—"

Ella stopped, as if somewhat at a loss. So Madge went on.

"I fired to let him know he was discovered. I believe the bullet lodged in the roof."

"Heavens! what a target."

"He took the hint, and did not wait to be made a target of himself."

"Then didn't you see him at all?"

"Through the window, as he was running down the road."

"Did you give the alarm?"

"We were in our night-dresses."

"Why, he might have murdered the two of you if he had liked."

"He might, but he didn't."

Madge's tone was dry. Ella put her hand up to her ears.

"Jack!—don't talk like that; I've been shivering ever since. You can't think what a day I've had in town, thinking of Madge in the house all alone."

"My dear girl." He put his arm about her waist, to comfort her. "And you think that it was—Graham's friend."

"It was Charles Ballingall."

This was Madge; Ella was less positive.

"My dear, how can you be so certain? You only caught a glimpse of the man's back in the darkness."

"He has committed burglary here before. His presence in the daytime is followed by another burglary that same night. Isn't the inference an obvious one? Don't you think so, Mr. Graham?

"It looks exceedingly suspicious. To convince a jury of his innocence he would have to prove an alibi."

"The burglar, whoever it was—and for the sake of argument we'll say that we don't know—took nothing with him, but he left something behind him, a piece of paper with writing on it. When the police came today—"

"Do you mean to say that the police have been here to-day?"

"Certainly—or, rather, a sample of them. And a lot of good he did, or is likely to do. I gave him the original piece of paper, but not before I had copied what was on it. Here is the copy. What do you make of it, Mr. Graham?"

Madge handed a sheet of paper to the gentleman addressed. As he looked at it Jack, too impatient to wait his turn, leaned over his elbow to look at it too.

"My stars! 'Tom Ossington's Ghost!' Large as life! Here's thrillers. What's that? 'Right—straight across— three four—up!' Here's mysteries! 'Right—cat—dog—cat—dog—cat—dog—dog—cat—dog—left eye,— push'—there seem to be several dogs after a good few cats. Perhaps it is my stupidity, but, while it's very interesting, I don't quite see what it means."

Madge paid no attention to Martyn. She kept her eyes fixed on his companion.

"What do you make of it, Mr. Graham?" she asked.

Bruce Graham continued silent for a moment longer, keeping his eyes fixed upon the paper. Then he looked up and met her glance.

"I think that we have here the key of the riddle, if we could only read it."

"If we could only read it!"

"Nor, from a superficial glance, should I imagine that that would be very difficult."

"Nor I."

"One thing it seems to me that this paper proves—that you were correct in your inference, and that last night's burglar was Charles Ballingall."

"I am sure of it."

"You two," interposed Martyn, "appear to be in thorough agreement—thorough! Which is the more delightful since you began by disagreeing. But you must excuse my saying that I don't quite see where the cause for harmony comes in."

"Are you so stupid?"

"My dear Madge! Don't strike me! It's constitutional."

"Don't you see what the situation really is?"

"Well—pardon me—but—really, you are so warm. Miss Brodie. If this gentleman were to allow me to study this interesting document, I might."

"Somewhere in this house, the dead man, Tom Ossington, concealed his fortune, all that he had worth having. It is as clear as if I saw the actual hiding place."

"My gracious goodness! Is it?"

"It is within a few feet of where we're standing. At this moment we're 'hot,' I know—I feel it!"

"Listen to that now! Madge, you must have second sight."

"That scrap of paper contains, as Mr. Graham puts it, the key of the riddle. It's a minute description of the precise whereabouts of the dead man's hiding place. All we have to do is to find out what it means, and if we are not all idiots, that shouldn't be hard. Why, you've only got to see the house; you've only to look about you, and use your eyes, to at once perceive that it's honeycombed with possible hiding places—just the sort of crevices and crannies which would commend themselves to such a man as this Tom Ossington. Look at this very room, for instance; it's wainscotted. That means, probably, that between the outer wall and the wainscot there's an open space—and who knows what beside? Listen!" She struck the wainscot in question with her open palm. "You can hear it has a hollow backing. Why"—she touched it again more gently, then stopped, as if puzzled—"why, the wood-work moves." She gave a little cry, "Ella."

"Madge?"

They came crowding round her, with eager faces.

CHAPTER IX

THE THING WHICH WAS HIDDEN

She had placed her hand against a portion of the wainscotting which was about level with her breast. As, in her excitement, she had unconsciously pressed it upwards, the panel had certainly moved. Between it and the wood below there was a cavity of perhaps a quarter of an inch.

"Push it! Push it higher!"

This was Jack. Apparently that was just what Madge was endeavouring to do, in vain.

"It won't move. It's stuck—or something."

Mr. Graham advanced.

"Allow me, perhaps I may manage."

She ceded to him her position. He placed his huge hand where her smaller one had been. He endeavoured his utmost to induce the panel to make a further movement.

"Put your fingers into the opening," suggested Jack, "and lever it."

Graham acted on the suggestion, without success. He examined the panel closely.

"If it were ever intended to go higher, the wood has either warped, or the groove in which it slides has become choked with dust."

Ella was peeping through the opening.

"There is something inside—there is, I don't know what it is, but there is something—I can see it. Oh, Mr. Graham, can't you get it open wider!"

"Here, here! let's get the poker; we'll try gentle persuasion."

Jack, forcing the point of the poker into the cavity, leant his weight upon the handle. There was a creaking sound—and nothing else.

"George! it's stiff! I'm putting on a pressure of about ten tons."

As he paused, preparatory to exerting greater force, Madge, brushing him aside, caught the poker from him. She drove the point against the wainscot with all her strength—once, twice, thrice. The wood was shivered into fragments.

"There! I think that's done the business."

So far as destroying the panel was concerned, it certainly had. Only splinters remained. The wall behind was left almost entirely bare. They pressed forward to see what the act of vandalism had disclosed.

Between the wainscot and the party-wall there was a space of two or three inches. Among the cobwebs and the dust there was plainly something—something which was itself so encrusted with a coating of dust as to make it difficult, without closer inspection, to tell plainly what it was.

Ella prevented Jack from making a grab at it.

"Let Madge take it—it's hers—she's the finder."

Madge, snatching at it with eager fingers, withdrew the something from its hiding-place.

"Covered," exclaimed Jack, "with the dust of centuries!"

"It's covered," returned the more practical Madge, "at any rate with the dust of a year or two."

She wiped it with a napkin which she took from the sideboard drawer.

"Why," cried Ella, "it's nothing but a sheet of paper."

Jack echoed her words.

"That's all—blue foolscap—folded in four."

Madge unfolded what indeed seemed nothing but a sheet of paper. The others craned their necks to see what it contained. In spite of them she managed to get a private peep at the contents, and then closed it hastily.

"Guess what it is," she said.

"A draft on the Bank of Elegance for a million sterling." This was Jack.

"I fancy it is some sort of legal document."

This was Graham. Ella declined to guess.

"Don't be so tiresome, Madge; tell us what it is?"

"Mr. Graham is right—it is a legal document. It's a will, the will of Thomas Ossington. At least I believe it is. If you'll give me breathing space I'll read it to you every word."

She drew herself away from them. When she was a little relieved of their too pressing importunities, she unfolded the paper slowly—with dramatic impressiveness.

"Listen—to a voice from the grave."

She read to them the contents of the document, in a voice which was a trifle shaky:—

"I give and bequeath, absolutely, this house, called Clover Cottage, which is my house, and all else in the world which at present is, or, in time to come, shall become my property, to the person who finds my fortune, which is hidden in this house, whoever the finder may chance to be.

"I desire that the said finder shall be the sole heir to all my worldly goods, and shall be at liberty to make such use of them as he or she may choose.

"I do this because I have no one else to whom to leave that of which I am possessed.

"I have neither kith nor kin—nor friend.

"My wife has left me, my friend has betrayed me; my child is dead.

"I am a lonely man.

"May my fortune bring more happiness to the finder than it has ever brought to me.

"God grant it.

"This is my last will and testament.

"(Signed) Thomas Ossington,

"October the twenty-second, 1892.

"In the presence of Edward John Hurley,   Solicitor's Clerk,   13, Hercules Buildings, Holborn. And of Louisa Broome,   2, Acacia Cottages, Battersea   (Maid-servant at present in the employ of the said Thomas Ossington)."

The reading was followed by silence, possibly the silence of amazement. The first observation came from Jack.

"By George!"

The next was Ella's.

"Dear life!"

For some reason, Madge's eyes were dim, and her tone still shaking.

"Isn't it a voice from the grave?" She looked down, biting her lower lip; then up again. "I th nk, Mr. Graham, this may be more in your line than ours."

She handed him the paper.

He read it. Without comment he passed it to Jack, who read it with Ella leaning over his shoulder. He placed it on the table, where they all four gathered round and looked at it.

The paper was stained here and there as with spots of damp. But these had in no way blurred the contents.

The words were as clear and legible as on the day they were written. The caligraphy was small and firm, and a little finical, but as easy to read as copperplate: the handwriting of a man who had taken his time, and who had been conscious that he was engaged on a weighty and a serious matter. The testator's signature was rather in contrast with the body of the document, and was bold and strong, as if he had desired that the witnesses should have no doubt about the fact that it was his name he was affixing.

Edward John Hurley's attestation was in a cramped legal hand, expressionless, while Louisa Broome's was large and straggling, the sign-manual of an uneducated woman.

Jack Martyn asked a question, addressed to Graham.

"Is it a will?—a valid one, I mean?"

"Looking at it on the surface, I should say certainly—if the witnesses can be produced to prove the signatures. Indeed, given certain circumstances, even that should not be necessary. The man expresses his wishes; their meaning is perfectly plain; he gives reasons for them. No testator need do more than that. What may seem the eccentric devising of his property is, in his position, easily accounted for, and is certainly consistent with entire sanity. Thousands of more eccentric documents have been held to be good in law. I have little doubt—if the testator's signature can be proved—that the will is as sound as if it had been drawn up by a bench of judges."

Madge drew a long breath. Jack was jocular, or meant to be. "Think of that, now!"

"But I don't see," said Ella, "that we're any forwarder now, or that we're any nearer to Madge's mysterious hoard. The will—if it is a will—says that the fortune is hidden in the house, but it doesn't give the faintest notion where. We might pull the whole place to pieces and then not find it."

"Suppose the whole affair is a practical joke?"

Mr. Graham commented on Jack's insinuation.

"I have been turning something over in my mind, and I think, Martyn, that I can bring certain facts to bear upon your supposition which will go far to show that it is unlikely that there is much in the nature of a practical joke about the matter. I want to call attention to Miss Brodie's copy of the paper which the burglar left behind last night—to the second line. Now observe." He crossed the room. "The paper says 'Right'—I have the door-post on my right, close to my right arm. The paper says 'straight across'—I walk straight across the room. Miss Brodie, have you a tape measure?"

Madge produced one which she ferreted out of a work-basket which was on a chair in a corner.

"The paper says 'three '—I measure three feet from where I am standing, along the wainscot—you see? It says 'four'—I measure four feet from the floor. As you perceive, that measurement brings us exactly to the panel behind which the will was hidden. The paper says 'up.' As Miss Brodie showed, there can be no doubt whatever that the panel was meant to move up. Owing to the efflux of time and to disuse, it had become jammed. Does not all this suggest that we have here an explanation of part of what was written on the burglar's paper?"

"It does, by George! Graham," cried Jack, "I always did know you had a knack of clarifying muddles. Your mental processes are as effective, in their way, as a handful of isinglass dropped into a cask of muddy beer. Ladies, I give you my word they are."

Martyn was ignored.

"If, therefore, part of the paper is capable of explanation of such a striking kind, does it not seem probable that the rest of it also has a meaning—a meaning which does not partake of the nature of a practical joke?"

"The idea," declared Madge, "of a practical joke is utter nonsense. As you say, everything points the other way. It is as clear as anything can be that, while one part of the paper is a key to the hiding-place of the will, the other is the key to the hiding-place of the fortune."

"Very well," said Jack. "Let's grant it. I stand snubbed. But perhaps you'll tell us what is the key to the key?"

"That's another question."

"Very much another question."

"But it needn't be an insoluble one, if we use our wits. The house isn't a large one; it isn't as though it contained a hundred rooms."

Mr. Graham had been studying the scrap of paper.

"This allusion to cats and dogs seems a striking one. I notice that each word is repeated five times. Is there anything about the house which gives you a hint as to the meaning?"

Madge replied to the question with another.

"Is there anything in this room which gives you a hint? Look around and see."

"I have been looking round, and I confess there isn't. Nor do I think it likely that the fortune would be hidden in the same room which contained the will."

"Very well; then we'll all of us go over the house together, and we'll all of us look out for hints."

Madge led the way, and they went over the house.

It was a tiny one. Behind the solitary sitting-room was the kitchen. The kitchen was an old-fashioned one, with brick floor, and bare brick walls coloured white. In one corner a door led into the pantry; in another was a door into the scullery; there was nothing remarkable about either of these. Under the staircase was a roomy cupboard. They examined it with some thoroughness, by the aid of a lamp, without discovering anything out of the way. On the floor above were the bedrooms used by Ella and Madge, and a smaller room in which they stored their lumber. The walls of these were papered from floor to ceiling, and in none of them did there seem to be anything calculated to convey a hint as to the meaning of the cabalistic allusion.

"It seems to me," observed Jack, when the work of exploration was completed, "that there's nothing about these premises breathing of either dogs or cats."

"It is just possible," said Graham, "that they may be in the grounds. For instance, several of them may be buried there, and the reference may be to one of their graves."

"Then do you propose to dig up the whole of the back garden till you light upon their hallowed bones?"

Graham smiled.

"I propose to do nothing."

Madge struck in.

"But I do; I mean to do a great deal. I'm going to strip all the wainscot off the sitting-room wall, and all the flooring up as well. And I'm going to continue that process till we reach the roof. I'm absolutely certain—absolutely certain, mind you!—that that unhappy man's hoard is somewhere within the four walls of this house, and I give you my word that I mean to find it."

"How about the landlord?" asked Graham. "What about his feelings? By the way, who is the landlord?"

"We're the landlord, Ella and I—or, at any rate, we very soon shall be."

"But in the meantime?"

"I don't know anything about a landlord. We took the house from Parker and Beading, the house agents over by the station."

"They would probably be acting for some principal. Did they not tell you his name?"

"They told us nothing. We took the house from them, and the supposition is that we're to pay the rent to them."

"If you will allow me, I'll take the will away with me—if you will trust me with it—and obtain expert opinion as to its validity. I will also call on Messrs. Parker and Beading, and ascertain, if possible, on whose authority they are acting."

"When will you do this?"

"The agents I will call upon to-morrow, and will acquaint you, by letter, with the result."

"You will do nothing of the kind—or, rather, I would prefer that you did not. Both Ella and I would prefer that you should come and tell us the result in person—that is if you can spare the time."

Mr. Graham bowed, expressing acquiescence in the lady's wishes. And on that understanding the matter was left.

When the two men had gone, Ella faced Madge with sparkling eyes.

"Suppose, Madge, there should be a fortune hidden somewhere in the house?"

Madge was scornful.

"Suppose!—there's no supposition about it. It's a certainty, I know there is."

"And suppose you should find it—it would be yours. What would you do with it?"

"What a question! We shall find it all four of us together. It will be share and share alike."

"What—Mr. Graham too?"

Possibly the question was put maliciously. It provoked Miss Brodie to wrath.

"Mr. Graham too? Ella, what can you mean? If it hadn't been for Mr. Graham we should have known nothing whatever about it. I suppose that, in strict equity, the whole of it would be his. Whatever can you mean by saying 'Mr. Graham too?' in such a tone as that!"

"My dear, I meant no harm. Really you're a trifle warm—don't you think you are?"

"Warm! It's enough to make any one a trifle warm to hear you talk like that."

Ella made a little face behind Miss Brodie's back.

"Well, fortune or no fortune, I do hope that no more burglars will come and look for it again to-night."

"If they do," declared Madge, with a viciousness which presaged violence, "they'll not find us unprepared. I shall sleep with Jack's revolver at my bedside, and if you like you can have half my bed again."

Ella's manner was much more mild.

"Thank you, my dear; since you're so good—I think I will."

CHAPTER X

MADGE FINDS HERSELF IN AN AWKWARD SITUATION

There was no burglar. The night was undisturbed; and the next day was, for both, a busy one.

The morning post brought Madge an intimation from a publisher to whom she had submitted one of her MSS., that he would be obliged if, when she was in town, she would call on him, so that she might discuss with him terms for its publication. That business-like memorandum made her heart beat faster; sent the blood coursing quickly through her veins; added a sparkle to her eyes. This, after all, was the sort of fortune she preferred—one for which she had striven with her own brains and hands—better than hidden hoards! The simple breakfast became an Elysian feast.

Ella was almost as jubilant as she herself was.

"Northcote & Co? That's a good house, isn't it?"

"Rather. They published—" Madge reeled off the names of two or three pronounced fictional successes.

"How much do you think they'll give you for it?"

"In cash?—not much; don't you think I shall bring home the Bank of England. So long as they give me a fair share of anything it may ultimately bring, I'll be content. But it isn't that; it's getting the first footing on the ladder—that's the thing."

"Of course it is. How splendid! And I'll tell you what; you shall dedicate it to me, and then if it sells by the hundred thousand, I shall have a bit of your fame."

"Done!—and your name upon the flyleaf ought to help to sell the book: it's as well known as mine is, anyhow. The author's spoken—you shall be the dedicatee?"

They went up to town together. Ella had to be at her office at half-past nine, and it is true that that seemed a trifle early to make a call upon a publisher. But, as Ella correctly observed, "You can look at the shops until it is time."

Which is precisely what Madge did do.

And it is remarkable how many things she saw in the shop windows which she mentally resolved to purchase if the book succeeded. Such an unusual number of useful things seemed to be displayed. And it certainly is odd what a quantity of them were just the articles which Ella and she particularly required.

Her interview with the publisher was a delightful one. She agreed to everything he proposed. His propositions were not quite on the scale of magnificence which she had conceived as being within the range of possibility. But still, they were near enough to be satisfactory. She was to have a sum of money paid her on the publication of the book—not a large sum, but still something. And there was to be royalty besides. When she hinted, almost as if she had been hinting at something of which she ought to be ashamed, that if part of the money were paid before publication it would be esteemed a favour, that publisher went so far as to draw a check for half the amount, and to hand it to her then and there. It is a fact that Madge Brodie was an uncommonly pretty girl—but such an accident was not likely to make any impression on the commercial instincts of a creature who battens upon authors.

She went straight off and cashed that cheque. When she had the coin in her pocket—actually in her pocket—she felt the financial equal of a Rothschild. She lunched all by herself at a restaurant in the neighbourhood of Charing Cross—and a nice little lunch she had; made some purchases, with one eye on Ella and another on herself; and then she went and gave a music lesson to Miss Clara Parkins, whose father is the proprietor of the Belvedere Tavern—that well-known hostelry, within a hundred miles of Wandsworth Common.

Miss Parkins was within a year or two of her own age, an uncommonly shrewd young woman, and a pleasant one to boot. The lesson had not been proceeding two minutes before she perceived that something was disturbing the ordinarily tranquil currents of her teacher's mind. When the lesson was finished, she made a valiant effort to find out what that something was.

She looked down, and she picked at the nap of her frock, and she asked, a tone or two under her usual key:

"What is it? I wish you'd tell me."

Madge stared; nothing which had gone before had led to such a question.

"What is what?"

"What is it which makes you—all brimming over?"

Madge went red. She was an arrant little snob, and by no means proud of giving music lessons to a publican's daughter—although that publican's daughter was the best paying pupil she had, and not the least agreeable. She was on her stilts in a moment.

"I don't understand you."

"That's a story. Of course it's no business of mine. But you do seem so happy, and I think that sharing other people's happiness is almost as good as being happy yourself—don't you? But I'm awfully sorry I asked."

Miss Parkins' air of contrition melted Madge's mood. As she adjusted her veil, she condescended to explain.

"I have had rather a stroke of luck."

"I'm awfully glad to hear it. Of course I know you think nothing of me; but I think no end of you. I do hope that some one has left you a fortune."

"I like it as well as if some one had, though I daresay you'll think it's nothing. I've sold a book."

"A book? Oh!—one of your own writing? I knew you were clever. When is it coming out?"

"We've hardly got so far as dates."

"When it does come, I'll buy a dozen and pay for them, if you'll give me one with your name inside."

"I'll give you the one without there being the necessity for your buying the dozen."

"I knew you'd say that. I know you don't think I'm good enough to buy your book. But I don't mind. I hope it will be a success."

"That's very kind of you."

"And it will be, I'm sure of it. You're the sort that does succeed."

"How do you make that out?"

"I don't know exactly—but you are. You've got the air of success about you. I noticed it when first I spoke to you. And when people have got the air of success, you'll generally find that they get the thing itself."

"You student of the world!"

She stooped and kissed the girl. It was the first familiarity they had exchanged. Miss Parkins put her arms about her neck and kissed her in return—a half quizzical something in her eyes.

"You mark my word—you're the sort that does succeed!"

Madge walked home with an added feeling of elation. She laughed at the girl's pretension to what almost amounted to prophetic insight—yet wondered if there might not be something in what she said. At any rate it was nice to be believed in, even by Miss Parkins. She felt that she had done the young woman an injustice. A publican's daughter, after all, is flesh and blood. If the book succeeded, should opportunity offer, she would place it upon public record that Clara Parkins had foretold its success—which would be fame for Clara. She smiled at her own conceit. The possibility that she might one day become an important person only loomed on the horizon since the advent of that note in the morning.

Immersed in such thoughts, almost unwittingly she arrived at Clover Cottage. Inserting her latchkey in the keyhole, she turned and opened the door. Almost as soon as she did so, it was thrust violently back on her, and banged in her face. She was so startled that, for a second or two, she stared at the closed door as if in doubt as to what had really happened. She had been, in imagination, so far away that it required positive effort on her part to bring herself back to earth.

"Well," she muttered, below her breath, "that's cool. I wonder who did that. Perhaps it was the wind."

She did not stay to consider how the wind could have behaved in such an eccentric manner. She gave her key another twist, and the door a push. But the key refused to act, or to move, in the direction required, and the door stood still. This, under the circumstances, singular behaviour of the key and the door, seemed to rouse her to a clearer perception of the situation. She gave the key a further twist, exerting all her strength.

"What is the matter? It turned easily enough just now."

It would not turn then, try how she might, and the door would not budge.

"Can the catch have fallen? I don't see how; it has never done anything of the kind before. I wonder if some one's having a joke with me; perhaps Ella has returned."

Acting on the supposition, though it was two hours in advance of the time at which Miss Duncan might be generally expected, she knocked at the door. None answered. She knocked again—louder. If Ella was having a jest at her expense it was hardly to be expected that she would put an end to the joke by answering her first summons. She knocked again and again—without result.

"This is charming—to be locked out of my own house is not what I expected."

She drew back, in order to survey the premises. Nothing was to be seen.

"Perhaps I'd better try the back door. Since the front seems hermetically closed, the back may be open for a change."

But it was not. She rattled at the handle; shook the door; rapped at the panels with her knuckles. No one heeded her. She returned to the front—with a curious feeling of discomfiture.

"What can have happened? It's very odd. The door opened easily enough at first—it felt as if some one had pulled it from within. I wonder—Hullo! that's the time of day is it? I saw that curtain move. I fancy now, Miss Ella Duncan, that I've caught you—you are amusing yourself inside. I'll give that knocker a hammering which I'll engage to say you shall hear."

She was as good as her word—so far as the hammering was concerned. She kept up a hideous tattoo for some three or four minutes without cessation. But though it is not impossible that the din was audible on the other side of the Common, within none heeded. She was becoming annoyed. Going to the sitting-room window, she tapped sharply at the frame.

"Ella, I saw you! Don't be so silly! Open the door! You'll have all the neighbourhood about the place. It's too bad of you to keep me outside like this."

It might be too bad; but the offender showed no sign of relenting. Madge struck her knuckles against the pane with force enough to break the glass.

"Ella!"

Still silence.

"How can you be so stupid—and unkind! Ella, open the door! Or is it you, Jack? Don't think I didn't see you, because I did—I saw you move the curtain."

She might have done, but the curtain was motionless enough now. Madge was losing her temper fast. In her estimation, to be kept out of the house like this was carrying a sufficiently bad joke a good deal too far.

"If you don't open the door at once, I shall break the glass and let myself in that way!"

She assailed the window-pane with a degree of violence which suggested that she meant what she said; then flattened her nose against it in an endeavour to discover who might be within. While she peered, the door was opened, and some one did come in. She started back.

"Who on earth—"

She was going to say. "Who on earth is that?" But when she got so far, she stopped—because she knew. At least in part.

First through the door there came a woman. And, although she could scarcely credit the evidence of her own eyesight, in her she recognised the visitor of the day but one before—the creature who had persisted in calling herself "the ghost's wife." At her heels there was a man, a perfect stranger to Madge. Having recognised the woman, she looked to see in her companion the loafer of the previous afternoon—but this certainly was not he. This was a miserable, insignificant-looking fellow, very much down at heel—and apparently very much down at everything else. The woman, with impudent assurance, came striding straight to the window. The man hung back, exhibiting in his bearing every symptom of marked discomfort.

The female, as brazen-faced as if she was on the right side of the window, stared at Madge. And Madge stared at her—amazed.

So amazed, indeed, that for a moment or two she was at a loss for words. When they came at last, they came in the form of an inquiry.

"What," she asked, "are you doing there?"

The woman waved her hand—in fact, she waved both her hands—as if repelling some noxious insect.

"Go away!" she cried; "go away! This house is mine—mine!"

Madge gasped. That the creature was mad, at the best, she made no doubt. But that conviction, in the present situation, was of small assistance. What was she to do?

As she asked herself this question, with no slight sense of helplessness, the gate clicked behind her. Some one entered the garden.

It was Bruce Graham.

CHAPTER XI

UNDER THE SPELL

"Mr. Graham!" she exclaimed. "Really, I do believe that if I had been asked what thing I most desired at this particular moment, I should have answered—you!"

Graham's sombre features were chastened by a smile.

"That's very good of you."

"Look here!" Laying one hand against his arm, with the other she pointed at the sitting-room window. His glance followed her finger-tips.

"Who's that?"

"That's what I should very much like to ascertain."

"I don't quite follow you. Do you mean that you don't know who she is?"

"I only know that I've been away all day, and that on my return I find her there. How she got there I can't say—but she seems determined to keep me out."

"You don't mean that! And have you no notion who the woman is? She looks half mad."

"I should think she must be quite mad. It's the woman who forced herself into the house the day before yesterday after you had gone—that's all I know of her. This time she is not alone; she has a man in there with her."

"A man! Not—Ballingall?"

"No, not Ballingall. At least, I only caught a glimpse of him—but it's not the man who was watching you. From her behaviour the woman must be perfectly insane."

"We'll soon make an end of her, insane or not."

Graham went to the window. The woman, completely unabashed, had remained right in front of it, an observant spectator of their proceedings. He spoke to her.

"Open the door at once!"

She repeated the gesture she had used to Madge—raising her voice, at the same time, to a shrill scream.

"Go away! go away! This house is mine—mine! I don't want any trespassers here."

Graham turned to Madge.

"Do you authorise me to gain an entry?"

"Certainly. I don't want to spend the night out here."

Permission was no sooner given than the thing was done. Grasping the upper sash of the window with both his hands, Graham brought it down with a run, tearing away the hasp from its fastening as if it had been so much thread. It was a capital object-lesson of the utility of such a safeguard against the wiles of a muscular burglar. The upper sash being lowered, in another moment the lower one was raised. Mr. Graham was in the room. The woman was possibly too astonished by the unceremonious nature of his proceedings to attempt any resistance, even had she felt disposed.

Graham addressed Miss Brodie through the window.

"Will you come this way? or shall I open the door?"

"If you wouldn't mind, I'd rather you opened the door."

He opened the door. Presently they were in the sitting-room, face to face with the intruders. Graham took them to task—the woman evincing no sign of discomposure.

"Who are you, and what is the meaning of your presence on these premises?"

"This house is mine—mine! It's all of it mine! And who are you, that you ask such a question—of a lady?"

She crossed her hands on her breast with an assumption of dignity which, in a woman of her figure and scarecrow-like appearance, was sufficiently ludicrous. Graham eyed her as if subjecting her to a mental appraisement. Then he turned to the man.

"And pray, sir, what explanation have you to offer of the felony you are committing?"

This man was a little, undergrown fellow, with sharp hatchet-shaped features, and bent and shrunken figure. He had on an old grey suit of clothes, which was three or four sizes too large for him, the trousers being turned up in a thick roll over the top of an oft-patched pair of side-spring boots. There was about him none of the assurance which marked the woman—the air of bravado which he attempted to wear fitted him as ill as his garments.

"I ain't committed no felony, not likely. She asked me to come to her house—so I come. She says to me, 'You come along o' me to my house, and I'll give you a bit of something to eat.' Now didn't you?"

"Certainly. I suppose a gentleman is allowed to visit a lady if she asks him."

The dreadful-looking woman, as she stood with her head thrown back, and her nose in the air, presented a picture of something which was meant for condescension, which was not without its pathos.

"Of course!—ain't that what I'm saying? She come here, and she took a key out of her pocket, and she put it in the keyhole, and she opened the door, all quite regular, and she says, 'This here's my house,' and she asked me to come in, so of course I come in."

"Do you mean to say that she gained entrance to this house by means of a key which she took from her pocket?"

"Course! How do you suppose we came in?—through the window? Not hardly, that's not my line, and so I tell you."

Graham returned to the woman.

"Be so good as to give me the key with which you obtained admission to these premises."

The woman put her hand up to her neck, for the first time showing signs of discomposure.

"The key?"

Starting back, she looked about her wildly, and broke into a series of shrill exclamations.

"The key!—my key!—no!—no!—no!—It is all I have left—the only thing I've got. I've kept it through everything—I've never parted from it once. I won't give it you—no!"

She came closer to him; glaring at him with terrible eyes.

"It's my key—mine! I took it with me when I went that night. He was sitting in here, and I came downstairs with the key in my pocket, and I went—and he never knew. And I've kept it ever since, because I've always said that one day when I went back I should want my key to let me in: I hate to have to stand on the step while they are letting me in."

Mr. Graham was regarding her intently, as if he was endeavouring to read what stood with her in the place of a soul.

"Is your name Ossington?"

"Ossington? Ossington?" She touched the sides of her forehead with the tips of her fingers, glancing about her affrightedly, as if making an effort to recall her surroundings. Her voice dropped to a whisper. "Who said Ossington? Who said it? Who asked if my name was—Ossington?"

Mr. Graham addressed Miss Brodie.

"With your permission I should like to speak to this woman—after the man has gone."

In his last words there was meaning.

"By all means, if you wish it. Get rid of him at once. At the best the fellow is an impudent intruder, and the story he tells is a ridiculously lame one. He must have been perfectly well aware that a woman of this sort was not likely to possess a house of her own, and that accepting what he calls her invitation he was committing felony."

The fellow in question shook his head as if he felt himself ill-used.

"I call that hard—cruel hard. If the young lady was to think of it for half a moment she'd see as it was cruel hard."

"The young lady declines to think of it. Have the goodness to take yourself away, and consider yourself lucky that you are allowed to escape scot free."

The man moved towards the door, endeavouring to bear himself as if he were doing so of his own free will. He spoke to the woman.

"Ain't you coming with me?"

"Yes, I'm coming."

She hastened towards him. Graham interposed.

"Let him go. There are one or two things about which we should like to speak to you, this young lady and I, after he has gone."

But she would have none of him. Shrinking back, she stared at him, in silence, for a second or two; then began to shriek at him like some wild creature.

"I won't stay!—I won't!—I shall go!—I shall! You tried to get my key—my key! You touch it—you dare! You asked me if my name"—she stopped, stared about as if in terror, gave a great sigh, "You asked me if my name—"

She stopped again—and sighed again, the pupils of her eyes dilating as she watched and listened for what was invisible and inaudible to all but her. Graham moved forward, intending to soothe her. Mistaking, apparently, his intention, she rushed at him with outstretched arms, giving utterance to yell after yell. In a moment she was past him and flying from the house.

Her male companion, who stood still in the doorway, pointed his thumb over his shoulder with a grin.

"There you are, you see—drove her out of her seven senses! So you have."

Much more leisurely, the man went after the woman.

For some reason, when Mr. Bruce Graham and Miss Brodie were left alone, nothing was said about the recent visitors.

"If you'll sit down and wait," remarked Miss Brodie, "I'll go and take my things off."

Having returned from performing those sacred offices, the topic still remained untouched. Possibly that was because there were so many things which needed doing. When one has been out all day, and keeps no maid, when one returns there are things which must be done. For instance, there was a fire to make. Miss Brodie observed that there ought to have been two, one in the kitchen, and one in the sitting-room; but declared that folks would have to be content with one.

And that one Bruce Graham made.

She brought in the wood, and the coal, and the paper; and then she went to fetch the matches. When she returned she caught him in the act.

"What are you doing?" she demanded.

He was on his knees on the hearthrug, with some sticks in his hand.

"Making a fire—on scientific principles. I'm a scientific expert at this kind of thing. Women's methods are unscientific as a rule."

"Indeed." Her air was scornful. "Men always think they can make fires. It's most surprising."

She commented on his methods—particularly when he took the pieces of coal from the scuttle, and placed them in their places with his fingers.

"That's right! Men always use their fingers to put coal on the fire—if they can. It's an agreeable habit."

He continued calm.

"It's scientific, strictly scientific; and may be logically defended, especially when a fire is being lighted. Heaping on coal with a shovel is unscientific—in the highest degree."

He struck a match; presently the paper was in flames.

"Now you had better go and wash your hands. You'll have to do it in the scullery; and by the time you're done, the fire will be out."

But the fire was not out. It was a complete success. The kettle was put on, preparations were made for tea, and the table was laid, Graham showing a talent for rendering assistance which was not accorded the thanks it might have been. Madge was chilly.

"I should imagine you were rather a handy person to have about the house."

"There are diversities of gifts; let us hope that each of us has at least one."

"Exactly. But, unfortunately, I do not care to see a man, what is called, 'making himself useful about the house'—if your gift lies in that direction. I suppose it is because I am not enough of a New Woman. Perhaps now you've given me your assistance in laying the cloth, you will give me some music."

He was smoothing a corner of the cloth in question—and looked down.

"It is you who are the teacher."

She flashed up at him.

"What do you mean by that?"

"It is true—is it not?"

"If you wish me to understand that you would rather not play, have the goodness to say so plainly."

Whereupon he sat down—and played. And Madge listened.

When he stopped, she was looking away from him, toward the fire. Tears were in her eyes.

"I suppose you are a genius?"

Her voice seemed a little strained. He shook his head.

"No—the music comes out of the ends of my fingers."

He went on playing. When he ceased, again she turned to him—with passionate eyes.

"I never heard any one play like you before."

"It's because I'm in the mood."

He played on. It seemed to her that he spoke to her out of the soul of music. She sat still and listened. Her heart-strings tightened, her pulses throbbed, her cheeks burned; every nerve in her frame was on the alert. Never had such things been said to her before. She could have cried—and would have cried, if she had dared. The message breathed to her by Bruce Graham's playing told of a world of which she, unconsciously, had dreamed.

He played; and she sat and listened, in the firelight, till Ella came home to tea.

And with Ella came Jack Martyn.

CHAPTER XII

TOM OSSINGTON'S LAWYER

It was while they were seated at table that Bruce Graham told them of the result of his investigations. Although, for some reason, the subject had not been mentioned when Madge and he had been alone together, that young lady showed herself alert and eager enough then. Nor, in that respect, was Ella behind her friend, while Martyn concealed an interest which was probably equal to theirs under ponderous attempts at jocularity.

It was Jack who brought him to the point.

"If the honourable and learned gentleman has sufficiently refreshed himself with the cup that cheers, would he oblige the company by mentioning if he has done anything in the matter of the Hidden Treasure—with capitals please!—and, if so, what?"

"I have at least found that everything points to there being such a hidden treasure—in spite of Jack's pretended scepticism."

"My pretended scepticism! Sir, I would have you know that I am no sceptic; or, if I am, never was one more willing to be converted to the faith."

Ella interposed.

"And, Mr. Graham, you really think there is a hidden treasure?"

"I think it extremely probable."

"Tell us all about it. What have you been doing? All day long I have been dreaming in the City of what would happen if we did light upon a secret hoard. It really would be too splendid for words."

The young lady looked the eagerness which the words suggested—like an imaginative child who pictures the materialisation of some favourite tale of faerie.

"To begin with, I went to the house agents to learn for whom they are acting."

"Well, and what did they say?"

"They were not particularly willing to say anything—as I expected. They were apparently under the impression that I intended to take the bread out of their mouths, by dealing with their principals direct. But when I had succeeded in, at any rate, partly reassuring them, they informed me they were acting for a firm of solicitors—Messrs. Nicholls & Hawkins, 3, South Square, Gray's Inn."

"Well, and what did you do then?"

"I went to the solicitors."

"It is awfully good of you to take so much trouble. And what did they say?"

"As it happened, I had some knowledge of the firm. My father was on terms of friendship with their senior partner, so that when I introduced myself to Mr. Nicholls as my father's son, the way was smoothed for me. They have the reputation of being a steady-going, old-fashioned firm, and I found them as open and above-board as they very well could have been. When I mentioned my errand, Mr. Nicholls was all alive at once."

"'Messrs. Palmer & Beading, of Wandsworth,' I began, 'inform me that in letting Clover Cottage they are instructed by you. May I ask who is the owner of the property?'

"When I said that, he sat up straight in his chair, and, as I observed, became all alive—oh.

"'May I inquire, in return, why you ask the question?'

"'The question,' I admitted, 'is a little irregular; but I take it that you will have no objection to give me an answer.'

"'Not the slightest. On the contrary, we shall be delighted if you will help us to throw light into what is, at present, a very dark corner; because, as a matter of fact, so far as we are concerned, there is no owner.'

"'The late Thomas Ossington died intestate!'

"'So far as our knowledge goes.'

"'Leaving instructions that you should act on his behalf?'

"'Not a bit of it. So far as we're aware, he left no instructions of any sort or kind. We have assumed a responsibility of which we should be glad to be rid. Do you know the man's history?'

"'I know something of it—though I confess, candidly, that I should like to know more. My own connection with the matter is a curious one. At a later stage I will tell you exactly what it is. In the interim, I assure you, on my word of honour, that any information you can give me shall be used for the furtherance of justice, and for that only.'

"'Very good; so long as right is done, all that we require is to be relieved of a very awkward situation. You know that Ossington was—peculiar?'

"'Not insane?'

"'Insane?—No; he was as sane as you are—every whit. But he was a disappointed man. He was malformed—the muscles of one leg were paralysed. As he grew older, the paralysis increased, until it extended up the whole of one side, and, at last, it killed him. He married a girl who acted as book-keeper at an hotel, at which he was in the habit of stopping, at Ilfracombe. She turned out a regular bad lot—finally running away with a man named Ballingall.'

"'Charles Ballingall?'

"'That's the man. Do you know him?'

"'I have acted for him professionally.'

"'Have you? Then let me inform you, without prejudice, that you have acted for as rascally a scamp as ever trod the earth. Ossington regarded him as a particular friend; and, as particular friends sometimes have a knack of doing, he borrowed no end of money from Ossington, ending by robbing him not only of his money, but of his wife as well. The double blow almost broke Ossington's heart, and during the remainder of his existence he lived the life of a recluse. But, until then, we had acted for him continually. For instance, we had acted for him in the purchase of Clover Cottage.'

"'Do you hold the deeds of the house?'

"'Not a deed. We hold nothing. All that we have are the various letters which he wrote to us at various times, on business. We had heard nothing of him for months, when one morning we received a telegram asking us to go at once to Clover Cottage. I went myself—I liked the man. He was, in his way, as fine a gentleman as I ever met. He had been cruelly used by friend and fortune. I found him dead—alone in the house there, with a maid and a doctor; dead—killed, according to the medical testimony, by a paralytic affection of the heart; but actually, as sure as you and I are alive, by the wicked wanton usage of those he had held dear. Now here the queer part of the thing comes in.

"'His last words had been an instruction to send for us; but that was the only instruction he had given. I myself searched the house from top to bottom, and, as you know, it is not a large one. I had it searched by others—every nook and cranny. Not a scrap of writing could be discovered—letter, note, or memorandum. Not a document of any sort of kind. Nothing whatever to show of what he had died possessed, or to whom it was to go.'

"'You had reasons to suppose that he had means?'

"'Every reason! We had every reason to believe him to be a man of comfortable means. We ourselves had, on more than one occasion, acted for him in matters involving thousands of pounds. We applied to the National and Provincial Bank—where we were aware he had an account. They informed us that he had closed the account some two months previously, and that on that occasion they had handed him over six thousand pounds in notes on the Bank of England. They gave us a list of the numbers of the notes; and not one of them has been presented for payment to this day.'

"'Is that so?'

"'It is. We furnished the Bank with a copy of the list, requesting them to notify us should one of them come in: as yet not a single one of them has made its appearance. Where are those notes? Surely, if they were in the possession of any living person, ere this some of them would have been presented. Where are the title deeds of Clover Cottage—and of other properties, of which he was the undoubted owner? He is the registered holder of ten thousand Great Northern Railway Stock. Since his death, the dividends on it have remained unclaimed. Where is the scrip? With the rest, has it vanished into air? In a box in his bedroom were forty-seven pounds in gold. That was all the cash the house contained. We buried him in Wandsworth Cemetery; Hawkins, I, and the doctor were the only mourners. We sold the furniture, paid the expenses, and the balance stands to the credit of the estate. We advertised for next of kin, without results. We advertised also for information as to the whereabouts of any property of which he might have died possessed—such as title-deeds, and anything of that kind. You understand that there is a delicate question as to who is entitled to collect the rents of other properties which we believe to have been his freehold. But nothing came of that. Clover Cottage we placed in the hands of Messrs. Parker and Beading, but only recently have they succeeded in letting it—I believe to two single ladies.'

"'So I understand.'"

Jack struck in.

"You are the two single ladies. You," pointing to Ella, "are one of them, and you," pointing to Madge, "are the other."

Ella was impatient.

"Jack, I do wish you wouldn't interrupt.—Mr. Graham, do go on. It's like a romance. My curiosity is such that I feel as if I were all pins and needles."

Bruce Graham continued.

"'And you, Mr. Nicholls,' I said, 'have you formed no theory of your own upon the subject?'

"Old Nicholls leaned back in his chair. He put his hands into his two pockets, and he looked at me out of the corners of his eyes.

"'I have—I have formed a decided theory. But, upon my word, I don't know what right you have to ask me.'

"'I trust, before we part, to prove to your entire satisfaction that I have every right. What's the nature of your theory?'

"'What's the nature of your right?'

"I laughed. I saw that he meant to understand more clearly where we stood before he went any further.

"'I believe I am in a position to produce an owner for the property—when found.'

"'When found?'

"'Precisely—when found. As yet it still remains to be found. I must ask you not, at this moment, to press me for further details, and of course you, on your part, are entitled to keep your theory to yourself.'

"'I am entitled to keep my theory to myself, as you say. But I know your father was an honest man, and as it happens, I know something about you, and I believe you also are an honest man. So as I am anxious, for many reasons, that this Ossington mystery should be unravelled, you shall have my theory for what it's worth.'

"'He tilted his chair on to its hind-legs, watching me keenly all the time.

"'Thomas Ossington was peculiar—not, in any sense of the word, insane, but out of the common run. In particular he was secretive, especially latterly, as perhaps was only natural. My theory is that, distrusting banks and all such human institutions, he secreted his cash, his title deeds, and everything he valued, in some hiding-place of his own contriving, and that there it remains concealed unto this hour.'"

The two girls rose simultaneously.

"Madge," cried Ella, "did you hear that? That's exactly what you said."

In Madge's tones there was the ring of an assured conviction.

"I was sure of it—and I am sure of it; as sure as any one possibly can be."

"May I ask," inquired Jack, with mock severity, "who is it who is interrupting now? Will you let the gentleman go on?"

Graham went on.

"'But where,' I said, 'do you think he is likely to have found such a hiding-place?'

"Old Nicholls looked at me, if possible, more shrewdly than ever.

"'At Clover Cottage. I knew the man. The salient events of his life happened there. In his whimsical way he regarded it as part and parcel of himself. I have heard him say so half a dozen times. His heart was in the place. Whatever he did conceal, was concealed within its four walls. Before the furniture was sold, I had it overhauled by an expert—some of the things were pulled to pieces. His verdict was that nothing was hidden there. Had I had my way I would have dismantled the whole house—only Hawkins was against me. He said very properly, that if the heir-at-law proved cantankerous, I might be made to smart in damages to the tune of a pretty penny. So I abstained. All the same, if the house was in the market to-morrow, I'd be a purchaser at a good round sum—if all rights of treasure trove went with it. You may tell the present tenants'—here he looked at me in a fashion which took me a little aback—'if you have the honour of their acquaintance, that we keep a sharp eye on the property; that it is not to be tampered with to the extent of one jot or tittle; and that not so much as one inch of paper is to be taken off the wall except with our express permission.'"

Ella turned to Madge.

"What do you say to that?" she exclaimed. "That knocks on the head all your notions of pulling the house to pieces."

Madge was defiant.

"Does it? It does nothing of the kind. Not after what I found in this very room last night. In the face of that, I care nothing for Mr. Nicholls, or for his threats either. What do you think yourself, Mr. Graham?"

"If you will allow me, I will give you my own opinion when I have told you of all that passed between Mr. Nicholls and myself. Indeed, I am now coming to that very point."

"There you are, you see. You will not let the man finish, you really won't. I never saw anything like you women for interrupting—never in all my life."

This of course was Jack—who was, as usual, ignored.

Graham brought his story to an end.

"'There is one more question', I said, 'which I should like to ask you, Mr. Nicholls. Do you know any one of the name of Edward John Hurley?'

"'I ought to, seeing that some one of the name of Edward John Hurley is in our office at this moment, and has been in our office for something over a quarter of a century.'

"'Can I see him?'

"Mr. Nicholls touched a bell, and presently Mr. Hurley entered. I felt that his presence on the spot was a stroke of luck for which I had certainly been unprepared. He was a tall, thin, dignified looking man, with grey hair. He wore spectacles. Taking them off, he wiped them with his handkerchief before he replaced them on his nose to look at me.

"'Do you remember, Mr. Hurley,' I began, 'the 22nd of October, 1892?'

"'The 22nd of October, 1892?' He repeated my words, then replied to my question with another, 'May I inquire why you ask?'

"'I will put my question in another form. Do you remember witnessing Mr. Thomas Ossington's attachment of his signature to a certain document on the 22nd of October, 1892?'

"I had noticed that Mr. Nicholls and he had exchanged glances when I first put my query. Now he looked at his principal evidently in search of guidance.

"'Shall I answer this gentleman's question, sir?'

"'Certainly. Give him all the information you can.'

"This Mr. Hurley proceeded to do, with the utmost clearness.

"'I do remember the 22nd of October, 1892, and the whole of the circumstances. I chanced to meet Mr. Ossington in Holborn as I was leaving the office. He asked me if I would dine with him in his house at Wandsworth. I went with him to dinner there and then. After dinner he asked me if I would witness his signature. I expressed my willingness. I witnessed it.'

"'Were you acquainted with the nature of the document he was signing?'

"'I was not. I have often wondered what it was, especially in the light of after events. The document, which was on a sheet of blue foolscap, had evidently been prepared before my arrival: Mr. Ossington, covering the writing with a piece of blotting-paper, signed it, in the middle of the page, directly underneath, while I affixed my signature, as witness, on the left-hand side.'

"'Was there another witness?'

"'There was, the servant girl.'

"'What was her name?'

"'I never heard it. I only know that he called her Louisa. I think I should recognise her if I saw her again. She was a red-faced, light-haired, strapping wench, about eighteen years of age.'

"'Should you recognise Ossington's signature—and your own—and the document to which they were attached?'

"'Most decidedly; under any circumstances, at any time.'

"I thanked him for his frankness, and rose to go. Nicholls stopped me.

"'One moment,' he said. 'Hurley informed us, at the time, of what he has just now told you, and, like him, we have frequently wondered what was the nature of the document he witnessed. As you are evidently aware that such a paper existed once upon a time, you are probably acquainted with its present whereabouts?'

"'I am. It will be produced in due course. When, I promise you, you will see as curious a document as is to be found upon the records.'

"Both Nicholls and Hurley endeavoured to induce me to be more definite. But I was not to be persuaded. Thanking them for the information they had given me, I came away."

CHAPTER XIII

AN INTERRUPTED TREASURE HUNT

"Well," inquired Martyn, when Graham? had finished, "what is the situation now?"

"First of all," struck in Madge, "how about the will?"

"As regards the will, I do not hesitate to say that it is as sound and valid a declaration of the testator's wishes as has been admitted to probate—Mr. Hurley's testimony removes all doubt upon that point. A man has a right to do what he will with his own—and that is all Mr. Ossington has done."

"How does it effect our right of search?"

"That is another question. The will gives neither you nor any one else a title for the destruction of property. It simply conveys to the finder the possession of certain things which are not specifically mentioned. But it authorises no one to look for those things, still less to do damage while looking."

"Then is our search barred? Aren't we to look at all?"

"I don't say that. My advice is to put the legal aspect aside, and to regard the common-sense one only. The will says that certain things, when found, are to become the property of the finder, and this house with them. You have reason to believe that those things are concealed within this house. Then it is for you to consider whether it is worth your while to run the risk of becoming responsible for any damage you may do in case of your failure to find those things. My opinion is, that it is worth your while to run that risk—that it is worth any one's while to run that risk."

Madge stood up, with resolute lips, and sparkling eyes. She struck her hand upon the table.

"I'm sure it is! I know it is!"

Bruce Graham also rose.

"I am willing to share the risk if it is shareable—or to assume the whole of it, for the matter of that. I incline strongly to your belief, Miss Brodie, that there is something hidden well worth the finding, and that its hiding-place is within the walls of Clover Cottage."

Jack Martyn hammered his fist upon the table.

"Hear, hear!—bravo!—spoken like a man! 'Pon my word, I'm beginning to think that there is something in it after all. A conviction is creeping over me, slowly but surely, that in less time than no time I shall be filling my pockets with the contents of Aladdin's Cave—and as there is only a bent sixpence and two bad pennies in them at present, there's plenty of room for more."

"The point is," said Ella, "where are you going to begin to look?"

"I am going to do what Mr. Nicholls wanted to do," declared Madge—"tear the house to pieces."

"But, my dear, even if you set about the business in that drastic fashion, you'll require method. How are you going to begin to take the house to pieces—by taking the slates off the roof, and the chimney-pots down?"

"And by taking the windows out of their frames, and the doors off their hinges, and displaying the grates in the front garden! George! you'll be improving the property with a vengeance if you do."

"I propose to do nothing so absurd. I simply wish you to understand that before I give up the search the house will literally have been torn to pieces—though I assure you, Ella, that I do not intend to begin by taking off either the slates or the chimney-pots."

"Have you been able to make anything more of the writing which was left behind by your burglarious visitor?"

The inquiry came from Graham. Madge shook her head.

"Let me try my hand at it," cried Jack. "I have brains—I place them at your service. It is true I never have been able to solve a puzzle from my very earliest hours, but that is no reason why I should not begin by solving this."

The scrap of paper was given him. He spread it out on the table in front of him. Leaning his head upon his hands, he stared at it, the expression on his face scarcely promising a prompt elucidation.

"The first part is simple, extremely simple. Especially after Mr. Graham's last night's lucid exposition. Otherwise I should have described it as recondite. But the second part's a howler; yes, a howler! 'Right—cat—dog—cat—dog—cat—dog—cat—dog—left eye— push!' The conjunction is surprising. I can only remark that if that assorted collection of animals is bottled up somewhere in this house all together, that alone would be a find worth coming upon. There will be some lively moments when you let the collection out."

"Did you mention anything to Mr. Nicholls about the paper?" asked Madge of Graham.

"Not a syllable. I gathered from what he said that the house was done up before it was let—papered, painted, and so on, and that therefore any former landmarks to which it might have been alluding have probably disappeared."

"That's what I think, and that's what I mean by saying we shall have to pull the house to pieces."

"Even if that is the case, as Miss Duncan puts it, where are you going to begin? You must remember that you will have to continue living in the house while it is being dismantled, and that you must spare yourselves as much discomfort as possible."

"It seems that you have to begin by pushing the left eye," said Jack, who still was studying the paper. "Though whether it is the left eye of the entire assorted collection is not quite clear. If that is the case, and that remarkable optic has to be pushed with any degree of vigour, I can only say that I shall take up a position in the centre of the road till the proceedings are concluded."

"Why not commence," asked Madge, "with a thorough examination of the room which we're now in?"

"You yourself," said Ella, "admitted last night that it was hardly likely that the treasure would be hidden in the same room which contained the will."

Madge pursed her lips and frowned.

"I've been thinking about that since, and I don't at all see why we should take it for granted. One thing's certain, the room is honeycombed with possible hiding-places. There are hollows behind the wainscot, the walls themselves sound hollow. That unhappy man can hardly have found a part of the house better adapted to his purpose."

"See there—what's that?" Ella was pointing to a kind of plaster cornice which ran round the room. "What are those things which are cut or moulded on that strip of beading, if it is beading, under the ceiling?"

"They look to me like some sort of ornamental bosses," said Graham.

"They certainly are neither cats or dogs," decided Madge.

"I'm not so sure of that; you know what extraordinary things they tell you are intended to represent things which are not in the least bit like them. Where's that paper? Jack, give me that paper."

Jack gave it her. She glanced at it.

"'Right'—I'll take up a position like you did last night, Mr. Graham, to the right of the door; 'cat—dog—cat—dog—cat—dog—cat—dog—' now—"

"Well?" queried Madge, for Ella had stopped. "Now what?"

"I think," continued Ella, with evident dubitation, "that I'll again do what you did last night, Mr. Graham, and cross right over; though it says nothing about it here, but perhaps that was omitted or purpose." She marched straight across the room. "Now we'll take the first thing upon the beading, or whatever it is, to be a cat, and we'll count them alternately—cat—dog—the fifth dog."

"Very good," said Graham, standing close up to the wall and pointing with his outstretched hand, "Cat—dog—cat—dog—cat—dog—cat—dog—here you are."

"Now, 'left eye—push.'"

"Or shove," suggested Jack.

"But there is no eye—whether left or otherwise."

"That's a detail," murmured Jack.

"Let me see." Ella clambered on to a chair. From that position of vantage she examined the protuberances in question.

"There really does seem nothing which could represent an eye; the things look more like knuckle-bones than anything else."

"What's the odds? Let's all get hammers and whack the whole jolly lot of them in the eye, or where, if right is right, it ought to be. And then, if nothing happens—and we'll hope to goodness nothing will—we'll whack 'em again."

"I'm afraid, Ella," put in Madge, "that your cats and dogs are merely suppositions. I vote, by way of doing something practical, that we start stripping the wainscot. You'll find hiding-places enough' behind that, and it's quite on the cards, something in them."

"Certainly," assented Jack, "I am on. Bring out your hatchets, pickaxes, crowbars, and other weapons of war, and we'll turn up our shirt-sleeves, and shiver our timbers, and not leave one splinter of wood adhering to another. Buck up, Graham! Take off your coat, my boy! You're going to begin to enjoy yourself at last, I give you my word."

Ella, possibly slightly exacerbated by the failure of her little suggestion, endeavoured to snub the exuberant Mr. Martyn.

"I don't know if you think you're funny, Jack, because you're only silly. If you can't be serious, perhaps you'd better go; then, if we do find something, you'll have no share."

"Upon my Sam!" cried Jack, "if that ain't bitter hard. If there's any sharing going on, I don't care what it is, if there's any man who wants his bit of it more than I do, I should like you to point him out. Ella, my dearest Ella, I do assure you, by the token of those peerless charms—"

"Jack, don't be silly."

"I think," insinuated Madge, "that you and I, Mr. Graham, had better go and fetch a chisel and a hammer."

They went. When they returned, bearing those useful implements, however the discussion might have gone, Mr. Martyn showed no signs of being crushed.

"Give me that chisel," he exclaimed. "You never saw a man handle a tool like me—and to the last day of your life you'll never see another. I'm capable of committing suicide while hammering in a tack."

"Thank you, Jack," said Madge; "but I think carpentering may be within the range of Mr. Graham's capacity rather than yours."

At least Mr. Graham showed himself capable of stripping the wainscot, though with the tools at his command—those being limited to the hammer and the chisel, with occasional help from the poker—it was not so easy a business as it might have been. It took some time. And, as none of the hoped-for results ensued—nothing being revealed except the wall behind—it became a trifle tedious. Eleven o'clock struck, and still a considerable portion of the wainscot was as before.

"Might I ask," inquired Jack, "if this is going to be an all night job; because I have to be at the office in the morning, and I should like to have some sleep before I start."

Graham surveyed the work of devastation.

"I will finish this side, and then I think, Miss Brodie, we might leave the rest to another time—till to-morrow, say."

"I really don't see what's the use of doing it at all," said Ella. "I don't believe there's anything hidden in this room; and look at the mess, it will take hours to clear it up. And who wants to live in a place with bare brick walls? It gives me the horrors to look at them."

Madge looked at her, more in sorrow than in anger.

"I think, Mr. Graham, that perhaps you had better stop."

He detected the mournful intonation.

"At any rate, I'll finish this side."

He continued to add to the uncomfortable appearance of the room; for there certainly was something in what Ella said.

He had worked for another quarter of an hour, or twenty minutes, and had torn off three or four more strips of wood—for they had been firmly secured in their places, and took some tearing—and the others were gathered round them, assisting and looking on, momentarily expecting that something would come to light better worth having than dust and cobwebs, of which articles there were very much more than sufficient, when Ella gave a sudden exclamation.

"Madge! Jack!" she cried. "Who—who's this man?"

"What man?" asked Madge.

Turning, she saw.

CHAPTER XIV

THE CAUSE OF THE INTERRUPTION

What she saw, and what they saw, spoke eloquently of the engrossed attention with which they had watched the work of destruction being carried on. So absorbed had they been in Bruce Graham's proceedings that, actually without their knowledge, a burglarious entry had been all but effected into the very room in which they were.

There was the proof before them.

The window had been raised, the blind and curtains pushed away, and a man's head and shoulders thrust inside.

When Ella's exclamation called their attention to the intruder's presence, they stared at him, as well they might, for a moment or two with stupefied amazement; the impudence of the act seemed almost to surpass the bounds of credibility. He, on his part, met their gaze with a degree of fortitude, not to say assurance, which was more than a little surprising.

To the fellow's character his looks bore evidence. The buttoning of his coat up to his chin failed to conceal the fact that his neck was bare, while the crushing of a dilapidated billycock down over his eyes served to throw into clearer relief his unshaven cheeks and hungry-looking eyes.

For the space of perhaps thirty seconds they looked at him, and he at them, in silence. Then Jack moved hastily forward.

"You're a cool hand!" he cried.

But Madge caught him by the arm.

"Don't!" she said. "This is the man who stared through the window."

Jack turned to her, bewildered.

"The man who stared through the window? What on earth do you mean?"

"Don't!" she repeated. "I think that Mr. Graham knows this man."

The man himself endorsed her supposition.

"Yes, I'm rather inclined to think that Mr. Graham does."

His voice was not a disagreeable one; not at all the sort of voice which one would have expected from a person of his appearance. He spoke, too, like an educated man, with, however, a strenuous something in his tone which suggested, in some occult fashion, the bitterness of a wild despair.

Seeing that he remained unanswered, he spoke again.

"What's more, if there is a cool hand it's Mr. Graham, it isn't me. I am a poor, starving, police-ridden devil, being hounded to hell, full pelt, by a hundred other devils—but, Bruce Graham, what are you?"

They turned to the man who was thus addressed.

At the moment of interruption he had been levering a strip of wainscot from its place with the aid of the inserted chisel. He still kept one hand upon the handle, holding the hammer with the other, while he drew his body back against the wall as close as it would go, and, with pallid cheeks and startled eyes, he stared at the intruder as if he had been some straggler from the spiritual world. From between his lips, which seemed to tremble, there came a single word—

"Ballingall!"

"Yes, Ballingall! That's my name. And what's yours—cur, hound, thief? By God! there have been people I've used badly enough in my time, but none worse than you've used me."

"You are mistaken."

"Am I? It looks like it. What are you doing here?"

"You know what I'm doing."

"By God! I do—you're right there. And it's because you know I know, that, although you're twice my size, and have got all the respectability and law of England at your back, you stand there shivering and shaking, afraid for your life at the sight of me."

"I am not afraid of you. I repeat that you are mistaken."

"And I say you lie—you are afraid of me, penniless, shoeless, hungry beggar though I am. Your face betrays you; look at him! Isn't there cowardice writ large?"

The man stretched out his arm, pointing to Graham with a dramatic gesture, which certainly did not tend to increase that gentleman's appearance of ease.

"Do you think I didn't see you the other day, knowing that the time was due for me to come out of gaol, trying to screw your courage to the striking point to play the traitor; how at the sight of me the blood turned to water in your veins? Deny it—lie if you can."

"I do not wish to deny it, nor do I propose to lie. I repeat, for the third time, that in the conclusions you draw you are mistaken. Miss Brodie, this is the person of whom I was telling you—Charles Ballingall."

"So you have told them of me, have you? And a pretty yarn you've spun, I bet my boots. Yes, madam, I am Charles Ballingall, lately out of Wandsworth Prison, sent there for committing burglary at this very place. My God, yes! this house of haunting memories of a thousand ghosts! I only came out the day before yesterday, and that same night I committed burglary again—here! And now I'm at it for the third time, driven to it—by a ghost! And, my God! he's behind me now."

A sudden curious change took place in the expression of the fellow's countenance. Partially withdrawing his head, he turned and looked behind him—as if constrained to the action against his will. His voice shrank to a hoarse whisper.

"Is that you, Tom Ossington?"

None replied.

Madge moved forward, quite calm, and, in her own peculiar fashion, stately, though she was a little white about the lips, and there was an odd something in her eyes.

"I think you had better come inside—and, if convenient, please moderate your language."

At the sound of her voice the man turned again, and stared.

"I beg your pardon. Were you speaking to me?"

"I was, and am. Mr. Graham has spoken to me of you, and I am quite certain that in doing so he has told us nothing but the exact and literal truth. In the light of what he has said, I know that I am giving expression to our common feeling in saying that we shall feel obliged to you if you will come in."

The man hesitated, fumbling with his hands, as if nonplussed.

"It's a good many years since I was spoken to like that."

"Possibly it's a good many years since you deserved to be spoken to like that. As a rule, that sort of speech is addressed to us to which we are entitled."

"That's true. By God, it is!"

"I believe I asked you to moderate your language."

"I beg your pardon; but it's a habit—of some standing."

"Then if that is the case, probably the time is come that it should die. Please let it die—if for this occasion only. Must I repeat my invitation, and press you to enter, in face of the eagerness to effect an entrance which it seems that you have already shown?"

Mr. Ballingall continued to exhibit signs of indecision.

"This isn't a trap, or anything of that kind?"

"I am afraid I hardly understand you. What do you mean by a trap?"

"Well"—his lips were distorted by what was possibly meant for a grin—"it doesn't want much understanding, when you come to think of it."

"We ask you to come in. If you accept our invitation you will of course be at liberty to go again whenever you please. We certainly shall make no effort to detain you, for any cause whatever."

"Well, if that's the case, it's a queer start, by—" He seemed about to utter his accustomed imprecation; then, catching her eyes, refrained, adding, in a different tone, "I think I will."

He did, passing first one leg over the sill, and then the other. When the whole of his body was in the room he removed his hat, the action effecting a distinct improvement in his appearance. The departure of the disreputable billycock disclosed the fact that his head was not by any means ill-shaped. One perceived that this had once been an intelligent man, whose intelligence was very far from being altogether a thing of the past. More, it suggested the probability of his having been good-looking. Nor did it need a keen observer to suspect that if he was shaven and shorn, combed and groomed, and his rags were exchanged for decent raiment, that there was still enough of manliness about him to render him sufficiently presentable. He was not yet of the hopelessly submerged; although just then he could scarcely have appeared to greater disadvantage. His clothes were the scourings of the ragman's bag—ill-fitting, torn, muddy. His boots were odd ones, whose gaping apertures revealed the sockless feet within. In his whole bearing there was that indefinable, furtive something which is the hall-mark of the wretch who hopes for nothing but an opportunity to snatch the wherewithal to stay the cravings of his belly, and who sees an enemy even in the creature who flings to him a careless dole. This atmosphere which was about him, of the outcast and the pariah, was heightened by the obvious fact that, at that very moment, he was hungry, hideously hungry. His eyes, now that they were more clearly seen, were wolfish. In their haste to begin their treasure-hunting they had not even waited to take away the tea-things. The man's glances were fastened on the fragments of food which were on the table, as if it was only by an effort of will that he was able to keep himself from pouncing on them like some famished animal.

Madge perceived the looks of longing.

"We are just going to have supper. You must join us. Then we can talk while we are eating. Ella, help me to get it ready. Sit down, Mr. Ballingall, I daresay you are tired—and perhaps you had better close the window. Ella and I shall not be long."

They made a curious trio, the three men, while the two girls made ready. Ballingall closed the window, with an air half sheepish, half defiant. Then placed himself upon a seat, in bolt upright fashion, as if doubtful of the chair's solidity. Jack took up a position in the centre of the hearthrug, so evidently at a loss for something appropriate to say as to make his incapacity almost pathetic—apparently the unusual character of the situation had tied his tongue into a double knot. Graham's attitude was more complex. The portion of the wainscot which he had undertaken to displace not having been entirely removed, resuming his unfinished task, he continued to wrench the boards from their fastenings as if intentionally oblivious of the new arrival's presence.

Nor was the meal which followed of a familiar type. The resources of the larder were not manifold, but all that it contained was placed upon the table. The pièce de resistance consisted of six boiled eggs.

"If you boil all those eggs," Ella declared, when Madge laid on them a predatory hand, "there'll be nothing left in the house for breakfast."

"The man is famished," retorted Madge with some inconsequence. "What does breakfast matter to us if the man is starving." So the six were boiled. And he ate them all. Indeed he ate all there was to eat—devoured would have been the more appropriate word. For he attacked his food with a voracity which it was not nice to witness, bolting it with a complete disregard to rules which suggest the advisability of preliminary mastication.

It was not until his wolf-like appetite was, at least, somewhat appeased by the consumption of nearly all the food that was on the table, that Madge approached the subject which was uppermost in all their thoughts.

"As I was saying, Mr. Ballingall, Mr. Graham has told us of all that passed between you."

At the moment he had a piece of bread in one hand and some cheese in the other—all the cheese that was left. The satisfaction of his appetite seemed to have increased his ferocity. Cramming both morsels into his mouth at once, he turned on her with a sort of half-choked snarl.

"Then what right had he to do that?"

"It seems to me that he had a good deal of right."

"How? Who's he? A lawyer out of a job, who comes and offers me his services. I'm his client. As his client I give him my confidence. Looking at it from the professional point of view only, what right has he to pass my confidence on to any one?—any one! He's been guilty of a dirty and disgraceful action, and he knows it. You know it, you do." He snarled across the board at Graham. "If I were to report him to the Law Society they'd take him off the rolls."

"I question it."

Madge's tone was dry.

"You may question it—but I know what I'm talking about. What use does he make of the confidence which he worms out of me?"

"I wormed nothing out of you." The interruption was Graham's. "Whatever you said to me was said spontaneously, without the slightest prompting on my part."

"What difference does that make?—Then what use does he make of what I said spontaneously? He knows that I am a poor driven devil, charged with a crime which I never committed. I explain to him how it happened that that crime comes to be laid against me, how I've been told that there's money waiting for me in a certain place, which is mine for the fetching, and how, when I went to fetch it, I was snapped for burglary. I'm found guilty of what I never did, and I get twelve months. In this country law and justice are two different things. What does my lawyer—my own lawyer, who pressed on me his services, mind!—do, while I'm in prison for what I never did? He takes advantage of my confidence, and without a word to me, or a hint of any sort, he goes and looks for my money—my money, mind!—on his own account—and for all I know he's got it in his pocket now."

"That he certainly has not."

This was Madge.

"Then it isn't his fault if he hasn't. Can you think of anything dirtier? not to speak of more unprofessional? Why one thief wouldn't behave to another thief like that—not if he was a touch above the carrion. Here have I, an innocent man, been rotting in gaol, think, think, thinking of what I'd do with the money when I did come out, and here was the man who ought to have been above suspicion, and whom I thought was above suspicion, plotting and planning all the time how he could rob me of what he very well knew was the only thing which could save me from the outer darkness of hell and of despair."

Graham motioned Madge to silence.

"One moment, Miss Brodie. You must not suppose, Mr. Ballingall, that because I suffer you to make your sweeping charges against me without interruption, that I admit their truth, or the justice of the epithets which you permit yourself to apply to me. On the contrary, I assert that your statements are for the most part wholly unjustifiable, and that where they appear to have some measure of justification, they are easily capable of complete explanation. Whatever you may continue to say I shall decline to argue with you here. If you will come to my rooms I will give you every explanation you can possibly desire."

"Yes, I daresay,—and take the earliest opportunity of handing me over to the first convenient copper. Unless I'm mistaken, that's the kind of man you are."

Madge caught the speaker by the sleeve of his ragged coat, with a glance at Graham, whose countenance had grown ominously black.

"If you will take my advice, Mr. Ballingall, since it is plain that you know nothing of the mind of man Mr. Graham really is, instead of continuing to talk in that extremely foolish fashion you will listen to what I have to say. The night before last we were the victims of an attempted burglary—"

"I did it—you know I did it. I give myself away—if there's any giving about it. You can whistle for a constable, and give me into charge right off; I'm willing. Perhaps it'll turn out to be the same bobby I handled before, and then he'll be happier than ever."

"I am sorry to learn that you were the burglar—very sorry. My friend, Miss Duncan, and I were alone in the house, a fact of which you were probably aware." That Mr. Ballingall might still be possessed of some remnants of saving grace was suggested by the fact that, at this point, he winced. "Other considerations aside, it was hardly a heroic action to break, at dead of night, into a lonely cottage, whose only inmates were a couple of unprotected girls."

"There was a revolver fired."

"As you say, there was a revolver fired—by me, at the ceiling. Does that tend to strengthen the evidence which goes to show that the deed, on your part, was a courageous one?"

"I never said that it was."

"You are perfectly conscious that we shall not whistle for a policeman, and that we shall not give you into charge. Is it necessary for you to talk as if you thought we should?"

"Am I to be robbed—"

"I fancy that the robbing has not been all upon one side." Mr. Ballingall did not look happier. "The burglar left behind him a scrap of paper—"

"Oh, I did, did I? I wondered where it was."

"At present it is in the possession of the police."

"The devil!"

"You need not be alarmed." Mr. Ballingall had suddenly risen, as if disturbed by some reflection. "That was before we knew by whom we had been favoured. Now that we do know, the paper will not be used in evidence against you—nor the police either. Before handing over that scrap of paper we took a copy of the writing which was on it. That writing was a key to two secret hiding-places which are contained within this house."

"How do you know that?"

"By exercising a little of my elementary common sense. Observe, Mr. Ballingall." Rising from her seat, she crossed to the door. "On that paper which you were so good as to leave behind you it was written, 'Right'—I stand on the right of the door. 'Straight across'—I walk straight across the room. 'Three'—I measure three feet horizontally. 'Four'—and four feet perpendicularly. 'Up'—I push the panel up; it opens, and I find that there is something within. That, Mr. Ballingall, is how I know the paper was a guide to two secret hiding-places—by discovering the first. What is the matter with the man? Has he gone mad?"

The question, which was asked with a sudden and striking change of tone, was induced by the singularity of Mr. Ballingall's demeanour. He had started when Madge took up her position at the door, eyeing her following evolutions speechlessly, breathlessly, as if spellbound. Her slightest movement seemed to possess for him some curious fascination. As she proceeded, his agitation increased; every nerve seemed strained so that he might not lose the smallest detail of all that happened, until when, with dramatic gestures, she imitated the action of striking the panel, raising it, and taking out something which was contained within, he broke into cry after cry.

"My God!—my God!—my God!" he repeated, over and over again.

Covering his face with his hands, as if he strove to guard his eyes against some terrible vision, he crouched in a sort of heap on the floor.

CHAPTER XV

THE COMPANION OF HIS SOLITUDE

When he looked up, it was timidly, doubtfully, as if fearful of what he might see. He glanced about him anxiously from side to side, as if in search of something or some one.

"Tom!—Tom!" he said, speaking it was difficult to say to whom.

He paused, as if for an answer. When none came, he drew himself upright gradually, inch by inch. They noticed how his lips were twitching, and how the whole of his body trembled. He passed his hand over his eyes, as a man might who is waking from a dream. Then he stretched it out in front of him, palm upwards, with a something of supplication in the action which lent pathos to the words he uttered—words which in themselves were more than sufficiently bizarre.

"Do any of you believe in ghosts?—in disembodied spirits assuming a corporeal shape?—in the dead returning from their graves? Or is a man who thinks he sees a ghost, who knows he sees a ghost, who knows that a ghost is a continual attendant of his waking and of his sleeping hours alike—must such a man be in labour with some horrible delusion of his senses? Is his brain of necessity unhinged? Must he of a certainty be mad?"

Not only was such an interrogation in itself remarkable, but more especially was it so as coming from such a figure as Ballingall presented. His rags and dirt were in strange contrast with his language. His words, chosen as it seemed with a nice precision, came from his lips with all the signs of practiced ease.

His manner, even his voice, assumed a touch of refinement which before it lacked. In him was displayed the spectacle of a man of talent and of parts encased in all the outward semblance of a creature of the kennel.

Madge, to whom the inquiry seemed to be more particularly addressed, replied to it with another.

"Why do you ask us such a question?"

About the man's earnestness, as he responded, there could be no doubt. The muscles of his face twitched as with St. Vitus' Dance; beads of sweat stood upon his brow; the intensity of his desire to give adequate expression to his thoughts seemed to hamper his powers of utterance.

"Because I want some one to help me—some one, God or man. Because, during the last year and more I have endured a continual agony to which I doubt if the pains of hell can be compared. Because things with me have come to such a pitch that it is only at times I know if I am dead or living, asleep or waking, mad or sane, myself or another."

He pointed to Graham.

"He has told you how it was with me aforetime; how I was haunted—driven by a ghost to gaol. When I was in gaol it was worse a thousandfold—I was haunted, always, day and night. The ghost of my old friend—the best friend man ever had—whom in so many ways I had so blackly and often wronged, was with me, continually, in my cell. Oh for some sign by which I could know that my sins have been forgiven me!—by which I could learn that by suffering I could atone for the evil I have done! Some sign, O Lord, some sign!"

He threw his hands above his head in a paroxysm of passion. As has been said of more than one great tragic actor, in his voice there were tears. As, indeed, there were in the eyes of at least one of those who heard. His manner, when he proceeded, was a little calmer—which very fact seemed to italicise the strangeness of his tale.

"The first day I spent in prison I was half beside myself with rage. I had done things for which I had merited punishment, even of man, and now that punishment had come, it was for something I had not done. The irony, as well as the injustice of it, made me nearly wild. I had my first taste of the crank—which is as miserable, as futile, and as irritating a mode of torture as was ever spewed out of a flesh and blood crank's unhealthy stomach; and I was having, what they called there, dinner, when the cell door opened, and—Tom Ossington came in. It was just after noon, in the broad day. He came right in front of me, and, leaning on his stick, he stood and watched me. I had not been thinking of him, and, a moment before, had been hot with fury, ready to dare or do anything; but, at the sight of him, the strength went out of me. My bones might have been made of jelly, they seemed so little able to support my body. There was nothing about him which was in the least suggestive of anything unusual. He was dressed in a short coat and felt hat, which were just like the coat and hats which he always had worn; and he had in his hand the identical stick which I had seen him carry perhaps a thousand times. If it was a ghost, then there are ghosts of clothes as well as of men. If it was an optical delusion, then there are more things in optics than are dreamt of in our philosophy. If it was an hallucination born of a disordered mind, then it is possible to become lunatic without being conscious of any preliminary sappings of the brain; and it is indeed but an invisible border line which divides the madmen from the sane.

"'Well, Charlie,' he said, in the quiet tones which I had known so well, 'so it's come to this. You made a bit of a mistake in coming when you did to fetch away that fortune of yours.'

"'It seems,' I said, 'as if I had.'

"He laughed—that gentle laugh of his which had always seemed to me to be so full of enjoyment.

"'Never mind, Charlie, you come another time. The fortune won't run away while you're in here.'

"With that, he turned and limped out of the cell; the door seeming to open before him at a touch of his hand, and shutting behind him as noiselessly as it had opened. It was only after he had gone that I realised what it was that I had seen. In an instant I was in a muck of sweat. While I was sitting on my stool, more dead than alive, the door opened again, this time with clatter and noise enough, and a warder appeared. He glared at me in a fashion which meant volumes.

"'Is that you talking in here? You'd better take care, my lad, or you'll make a bad beginning.'

"He banged the door behind him—and he went."

Ballingall paused, to wipe his brow with the back of his hand; and he sighed.

"I made a bad beginning, and, from the warder's point of view, I went from bad to worse. I do not know if the man I had injured has been suffered to torture me before my time, or if, where he is, his nature has changed, and he seeks, in the grave, the vengeance he never sought in life. If so, he has his fill of it— he surely has had his fill of it!—already. It was through him that I was there, and now that I was there he made my sojourn in the prison worse than it need have been. Much worse, God knows.

"That first visitation of his was followed by others. Twice, thrice, sometimes four times a day, he would come to me when I was in my cell, and speak to me, and compel me to answer him; and my voice would be heard without. It became quite a custom for the warder on duty to stand outside my cell, often in the middle of the night, and pounce on me as soon as Tom had gone. The instant Tom went, the warder would come in. Never once did an officer enter while he was actually with me, but, almost invariably, his departure was the signal for the warder to put in his appearance. I don't know how it was, or why it was, but so it was. I would be accused of carrying on a conversation with myself, reported, and punished. As a matter of fact, I was in continual hot water—because of Tom. Not a single week passed from that in which I entered the prison, to that in which I left it, during which I did not undergo punishment of some sort or the other, because of Tom. As a result, all my marks were bad marks. When I left the gaol, so far from receiving the miserable pittance which good-conduct prisoners are supposed to earn, I was penniless; I had not even the wherewithal with which to buy myself a crust of bread.

"A more dreadful form of torture Tom could hardly have invented. A man need not necessarily suffer although he is in gaol. But I suffered. Always I was in the bad books of the officers. They regarded me as an incorrigible bad-conduct man—which, from their point of view, I was. All sorts of ignominy was heaped on me. Every form of punishment I could be made to undergo I had to undergo. I never earned my stripe, nor the right of having a coir mattress with which to cover the bare board on which I was supposed to sleep. I was nearly starved, owing to the perpetually recurring bread and water. And the horrors I endured, the devils which beset me, in that unspeakable dark cell! To me, gaol was a long-drawn-out and ever-increasing agony, from the first moment to the last.

"God knows it was!"

The speaker paused. He stood, his fists clenched, staring vacantly in front of him, as if he saw there, in a mist, the crowding spectres of the past. There seemed to come a break in his voice as he continued. He spoke with greater hesitation.

"Some three months before my sentence was completed, Tom changed his tactics. While I was sleeping—such sleep!—on the bare board which served me as a bed, I'd have a vision. It was like a vision—like a vision, and yet—it was as if I was awake. It seemed as if Tom came to me, and put his arm into mine, and led me out of gaol, and brought me here to Clover Cottage. He'd stand at the gate and say 'Charlie, this is Clover Cottage,' and I'd answer, 'I know it is.' Then he'd laugh—in some way that laugh of his seemed to cut me like a knife. And he'd lead me down the pathway and into the house, to this very room. Though"—Ballingall looked about him doubtfully—"it wasn't furnished as it is now. It was like it used to be. And he'd go and stand by the door, as you did"—this was to Madge—"and he'd say, 'Now, Charlie, pay particular attention to what I am about to do. I'm going to show you how to get that fortune of yours—which you came for once before and went away without. Now observe.'

"Then he'd walk straight across the room, as you did," again to Madge—"and he'd turn to me and say, 'Notice exactly what I'm doing!' Then he'd take a foot rule from his pocket, and he'd measure three feet from where he stood along the floor. And he'd hold up the rule, and say, 'You see—three feet.' Then he'd measure four feet from the floor, and hold out the rule again and say, 'You see, four feet.' Then he'd put his hand against the panel and move it upwards, and it would slide open—and there was an open space within. He'd put his hand into the open space, and take something out; it looked to me like a sheet of paper. And he'd say, 'This is what will give you that fortune of yours—when you find it. Only you'll have to find it first. Be sure you find it, Charlie.'

"And he'd laugh—and, though it was the gentle laugh of his which I had known so well of old, there was something about it which seemed to mock me, and cut me like a whip and make me quiver. He'd take my arm again, and lead me from the house and back to the gaol, and I'd wake to find myself lying on the bare board, alone in the dark cell, crying like a child.

"In the morning, perhaps at dinner-time, he'd come into the cell in the usual way, and ask me:

"'Charlie, do you remember last night?' 'Yes, Tom,' I'd reply, 'I do.' And then he'd go on:

"'Mind you don't forget. It's most important, Charlie, that you shouldn't forget. I'll tell you what you must remember. Take this and write it down.'

"And he'd give me something, my Bible, or my prayer-book, or even the card of rules which was hung against the wall, and a piece of pencil—though where he got that from I never knew, and he'd say, 'Now write what I dictate.'

"And I did, just as you saw it on the paper which I left behind; the first line, 'Tom Ossington's Ghost'—he always made me write that; it was the only allusion he ever made to there being anything unusual about his presence there; and the second line, 'right—straight across—three—four—up.' When I'd written it he'd say:

"'Charlie, mind you take the greatest care of that; don't let it go out of your possession for a moment. It's the guide to that fortune of yours.'

"Then he'd go. And the moment he had gone the warder would come bursting in, and catch me with the pencil, and the Bible, or whatever it was, in my hand, with the writing on the flyleaf. And he'd begin to gird at me.

"'So you're at it again, are you? And you've got a pencil, have you? and been writing in your Bible? You're a pretty sort, upon my word you are. I tell you what it is, my lad, you'll get yourself into serious trouble before you've done.'

"And he'd take the pencil away with him, and the Bible, and the writing; and I'd be reported again, and punished with the utmost severity which was within the compass of the Governor's power."

Ballingall stopped again. A convulsive fit of trembling seemed to go all over him.

"Towards the end, the vision took another form. Tom would bring me to the house—only I think, not to this room, but to another—and he would do something—he would do something. I saw quite clearly what it was he did, and understood it well, but, so soon as I was out of the house, the recollection of what he had done became blurred as by a mist. I could not remember at all. I'd wake in my cell in an agony to think that all that Tom had shown me should have slipped my memory. In the morning he'd come and ask:

"'Charlie, you remember what we did last night?'

"'No, Tom, I don't. I've tried to think, but I can't. It's all forgotten.'

"He'd laugh—his laugh seeming to mock me more than ever.

"'Never mind, Charlie, I'll tell you all about it. You write down what I say.'

"And I wrote it down—the last line which was on the scrap of paper. Though I never knew what it meant—never! never! I've searched my brains many times to think; and been punished for writing it again and again.

"At last I was released. At last—my God, at last!"

His whole frame quivered. He drew himself upright, as if endeavouring to bear himself as became a man.

"I was treated, when going out, according to my deserts. I had earned no favour, and I received none. The Governor reprimanded me, by way of a God-speed; told me that my conduct, while in prison, had been very bad, and warned me that it would go ill with me if I returned. I went out in the rags in which I had entered, without a penny in my pocket—hungry at the moment of release, I have not tasted bite or sup from the time that I came out of gaol until tonight.

"In the afternoon I came round to Clover Cottage. The first thing I saw was him." He pointed to Graham. "He was afraid of me, and I was afraid of him—that is the truth. Otherwise I should have gone up to him and asked him for at least a shilling, because directly I caught sight of him I knew what he was after, and that I was going to be tricked and robbed again. While I was trying to summon up courage enough to beg of the man whom I knew had played me false, I saw some one else, and I ran away.

"I meant to get a bed in the casual ward of the Wandsworth Workhouse. But Tom came to me as I was going there, and told me not to be so silly, but to come and get the fortune which was waiting for me at Clover Cottage. So I came. But I never got the fortune.

"And ever since I've been growing hungrier and hungrier, until I've grown beside myself with hunger— because Tom stopped me when I was going to the workhouse again last night, and bade me not to be so silly, though I don't know why I should have been silly in seeking for shelter and for food. And not a couple of hours ago he came to me while I was trying to find a hole on the Common in which to sleep, and packed me off once more to fetch away my fortune. But I haven't found it yet—not yet, not yet. Though"—he stretched out his arms on either side of him, and on his face there came a strange look of what seemed exultation—"I know it's near."

In the pause which followed, Ella raised her hand.

"Listen," she exclaimed; "who's that? There's some one at the garden gate."

There did seem some one at the garden gate, some one who opened and shut it with a bang. They heard footsteps on the tiles which led to the front door. While they waited, listening for a knock, another sound was heard.

"Hark," cried Ella. "There's some one fumbling with a latchkey at the door, trying to open t. Whoever can it be—at this hour of the night? There must be some mistake."

"I think," said Madge, in her eyes there was a very odd expression, "it is possible there is no mistake— this time."

CHAPTER XVI

TWO VISITORS

Instinctively Ella drew closer to Jack, nestling at his side, as if for the sake of the near neighbourhood. Graham advanced towards Madge, placing himself just at her back, with a something protective in his air—as if he designed to place himself in front of her at an instant's warning. While Ballingall moved farther towards the window, with that in his bearing which curiously suggested the bristling hairs of the perturbed and anxious terrier. And all was still—with that sort of silence which is pregnant with meaning.

Without in the stillness, there could be plainly heard the fumbling of the latchkey, as if some one, with unaccustomed hands, was attempting to insert it in the door. Presently, the aperture being found, and the key turned, the door was opened. Some one entered the house; and, being in, the door was shut— with a bang which seemed to ring threateningly through the little house, causing the listeners to start. Some one moved, with uncertain steps, along the passage. A grasp was laid from without on the handle of the sitting-room door. They saw it turn. The door opened—while those within, with one accord, held their breath. And there entered as strange and pitiful a figure as was ever seen.

It was the "ghost's wife," the woman who had so troubled Madge, who had done her best that afternoon to keep her outside the house. She was the saddest sight in her parti-coloured rags, the dreadful relics of gaudy fripperies.

When they saw it was her, there was a simultaneous half-movement, which never became a whole movement, for it was stopped at its initiatory stage—stopped by something which was in the woman's face, and by the doubt if she was alone.

On her face—her poor, dirty, degraded, wrinkled face—which was so pitifully thin there was nothing left of it but skin and bone, there was a look which held them dumb. It was a look like nothing which any of them had ever seen before. It was not only that it was a look of death—for it was plain that the outstretched fingers of the angel already touched her brow; but it was the look of one who seemed to see beyond the grave—such a look as we might fancy on the face of the dead in that sudden shock of vision which, as some tell us, comes in the moment after death.

She was gazing straight in front of her, as if at some one who was there; and she said, in the queerest, shakiest voice:

"So, Tom, you've brought me home at last. I'm glad to be at home again. Oh, Tom!" This last with the strangest catching in her throat. She looked about her with eyes that did not see. "It seems a long time since I was at home. I thought I never should come back—never! After all, there's nothing to a woman like her home—nothing, Tom." Again there was that strange catching. "You've brought me a long way— a long, long way. To think that you should see me in the Borough—after all these years—and should bring me right straight home, I wondered, if ever you did see me, if you'd bring me home—Tom. Only I wish—I wish you'd seen me before. I'm—a little tired now."

She put her hand up to her face with a gesture which suggested weariness which was more than mortal, and which only eternal rest could soothe—her hand in what was once a glove. When she removed it there was something in her eyes which showed that she had suddenly attained to at least a partial consciousness of her surroundings. She looked at the two girls and the two men grasped together on her right, with, at any rate, a perception that they were there.

"Who—who are these people? Whoever you are, I'm glad to see you; this is a great night with me. I've seen my husband for the first time for years and years, and he's brought me home with him again—after all that time. This is my husband—Tom."

She held out her hand, as if designating with it some one who was in front of her. They, on their part, were silent, spellbound, uncertain whether the person to whom and of whom she spoke with so much confidence might not be present, though by them unseen.

"It's a strange homecoming, is it not? And though I'm tired—oh, so tired!—I'm glad I'm home again. To this house he brought me when we were married—didn't you, Tom? In this house my baby was born— wasn't it, Tom? And here it died." There came a look into her face which, for the moment, made it beautiful; to such an extent is beauty a matter of expression. "My dear little baby! It seems only the other day when I held it in my arms. It's as if the house were full of ghosts—isn't it, Tom?"

Her eyes wandered round the room, as if in search of some one or of something, and presently they lighted upon Mr. Ballingall. As they did so, the whole expression of her countenance was changed; it assumed a look of unspeakable horror.

"Charles Ballingall!" she gasped. "Tom—Tom, what is he doing here?"

She stretched out her hands, seeming to seek for protection from the some one who was in front of her—repeating the other's name as if involuntarily, as though it were a thing accursed.

"Charles Ballingall!"

Slowly, inch by inch, her glance passed from the shrinking vagabond, until it stayed, seeming to search with an eager longing the face of the one who was before her in the apparently vacant air.

"Tom!—what's he doing here? Tom! Tom! don't look at me like that! Don't, Tom—for God's sake, don't look at me like that!" She broke into sudden volubility, every word a cry of pain. "Tom, I'm—I'm your wife! You—you brought me home! Just now!—from the Borough!—all the way!—all the long, long way—home! Tom!"

The utterance of the name was like a scream of a wounded animal in its mortal agony.

The four onlookers witnessed an extraordinary spectacle. They saw this tattered, drabbled remnant of what was once a woman, whose whole appearance spoke of one who tottered on the very borders of the grave, struggling with the frenzy of an hysterical despair with the visitant from the world of shades who, it was plain to her, if not to others, was her companion—the husband whom, with such malignant cruelty and such persistent ingratitude, she had wronged so long ago. She had held out her hands, her treacherous hands, seeking to shelter them in his; and it seemed as if, for a moment, he had suffered them to stay, and that now, since she had realised the presence of her associate in sin, unwilling to retain them any more in his, he sought to thrust them from him; while she, perceiving that what she had supposed to be the realisation of hopes which she had not even dared to cherish was proving but a chimera, and the fruit which she was already pressing to her lips but an Apple of Sodom, strained every nerve to retain the hold of the hands whose touch had meant to her almost an equivalent to an open door to Paradise. With little broken cries and gasping supplications, she writhed and twisted as she strove to keep her grasp.

"Tom! Tom! Tom!" she exclaimed, over and over again. "You brought me home! you brought me home! Don't put me from you! Tom! Tom! Tom!"

It seemed that the struggle ended in her discomfiture, and that the hands which she had hoped would draw her forward had been used to thrust her back; for, staggering backwards as if she had been pushed, she put her palms up to her breasts and panted, staring like one distraught.

By degrees, regaining something of her composure, she turned and looked at Ballingall, with a look before which he cowered, actually raising his arm as if warding off a blow. And, when she had breath enough, she spoke to him, in a whisper, as if her strength was gone.

"What are you doing here?"

Ballingall hesitated, looking about him this way and that as if seeking for some road of retreat. Finding none, making a pitiful effort to gather himself together, he replied to her question in a voice which was at once tremulous and sullen.

"Tom asked me to come. You know, Tom, you asked me to come."

He stretched out his arm with a gesture which was startling, as if to him also the woman's companion was a reality. There was silence. He repeated his assertion, still with his outstretched arm.

"You know, Tom, you asked me to come."

Then there happened the most startling thing of all. Some one laughed. It was a man's laugh—low, soft, and musical. But there was about it this peculiar quality—it was not the merriment of one who laughs with, but of one who laughs at; as though the laugher was enjoying thoroughly, with all his heart, a jest at another's expense. Before it the man and woman cowered, as if beneath a rain of blows.

After it ceased they were still. It was plain that the woman was ashamed, disillusioned, conscious that she had been made a butt of; and that, in spite of all appearances to the contrary, she was still among the hopeless, the outcast, the condemned. She glanced furtively towards the companion of her shame; then more quickly still away from him, as if realising only too well that, in that quarter, there was no promise of hope rekindled. And she said, with choking utterance:

"Tom, I never thought—you'd laugh at me. Did you bring—me home—for this?"

She put up her hands, in their dreadful gloves, to her raddled, shrunken face, and stood, for a moment, still. Then her frame began to quiver, and she cried; and as she cried there came that laugh again.

The note of mockery that was in it served to sting Ballingall into an assertion of such manhood as was in him. He clenched his fists, drew himself straighter, and, throwing back his head, faced towards where the laughter seemed to stand.

"Tom," he said, "I've used you ill. We've both of us used you ill, both she and I—she's been as false a wife to you as I've been friend. Our sins have been many—black as ink, bitter as gall. We know it, both of us. We've had reason to know it well. But, Tom, consider what our punishment has been. Look at us—at her, at me. Think of what we were, and what we are. Remember what it means to have come to this from that. Every form of suffering I do believe we've known—of mind and of body too—she in her way, and I in mine. We've been sinking lower and lower and lower, through every form of degradation, privation, misery, until at last we're in the ditch—amidst the slime of the outer ditch. We've lost all that there is worth having, so far as life's concerned, for ever. The only hope that is left us is the hour in which it is appointed that we shall die. For my part, my hope is that for me that hour is not far off. And, as I'm a living man, I believe that for her it has already come; that the scythe is raised to reap; that she's dying where she stands. Have you no bowels of compassion, Tom—none? You used to have. Are they all dried and withered? There's forgiveness for sinners, Tom, with God; is there none with you? You used to be of those who forgive till seventy times seven; are you now so unforgiving? You may spurn me, you may trample on me, you may press my head down into the very slime of the ditch; you know that these many months you've torn and racked me with all the engines of the torture chambers: but she's your wife, Tom—she was your wife! you loved her once! She bore to you a little child—a little baby, Tom, a little baby! It's dead—with God, Tom, with God! She's going to it now—now, now! While she's passing into the very presence chamber, where her baby is, don't abase her, Tom. Don't, Tom, don't!"

He threw out his arms with a gesture of such frenzied entreaty, and his whole figure was so transformed by the earnestness, and passion, and pathos, and even anguish with which he pressed his theme, that at least the spectators were cut to the heart.

"I know not," he cried, "whether you are dead or living, or whether I myself am mad or sane—for, indeed, to me of late the world has seemed all upside down. But this I know, that I see you and that you see me, and if, as I suppose, you come from communion with the Eternal, you must know that, in that Presence, there is mercy for the lowest—for the chief of sinners! There is mercy, Tom, I know that there is mercy! Therefore I entreat you to consider, Tom, the case of this woman—of she who was your wife, the mother of your child. She has paid dearly for her offence against you—paid for it every moment of every hour of every day of every year since she offended. Since then she has been continually paying. Is not a quittance nearly due—from you, Tom? If blood is needed to wash out her guilt, she has wept tears of blood. If suffering—look at her and see how she has suffered. And now, even as I stand and speak to you, she dies. She bears her burden to the grave. Is she to add to it, still, the weight of your resentment? That will be the heaviest weight of all. Beneath it, how shall she stagger to the footstool of her God? All these years she has lived in hell. Don't—with your hand, Tom!—now she's dying, thrust her into hell, for ever. But put her hand in yours, and bear her up, and stay her, Tom, and lead her to the throne of God. If she can say that you've forgiven her, God will forgive her too. And then she'll find her baby, Tom."

It was a strange farrago of words which Ballingall had strung together, but the occasion was a strange one too. His earnestness, in which all was forgotten save his desire to effect his purpose, seemed to cast about them a halo as of sanctity. It was almost as if he stood there, pleading for a sinner, in the very Name of Christ—the great Pleader for all great sinners.

The woman, this latest Magdalene, did as that first Magdalene had done, she fell on her knees and wept—tears of bitterness.

"Tom! Tom!" she cried, "Tom! Tom!"

But he to whom she cried did not do as the Christ, the Impersonation of Divine Mercy, did. Christ wept with the sinners. He to whom she pleaded laughed at her. And, beneath his laughter, she crouched lower and lower, till she lay almost prostrate on the floor; and her body quivered as if he struck her with a whip.

Ballingall, as if he could scarcely credit the evidence of his own senses, started back and stared, as though divided between amazement and dismay. Under his breath, he put a singular inquiry—the words seeming to be wrung from him against his will.

"Tom!—Are you a devil?"

And it seemed as if an answer came. For he stood in the attitude of one who listens, and the muscles of his face worked as if what was being said was little to his mind. A dogged look came into his eyes, and about his mouth. He drew himself further back, as if retreating before undesired advances. Words came sullenly from between his teeth.

"No, Tom, no—I want none of that. It isn't that I ask; you know it isn't that."

It appeared as if the overtures made by the unseen presence, unwelcome though they were, were being persisted in. For Ballingall shook his head, raising his hands as if to put them from him, conveying in his bearing the whole gamut of dissent; breaking, at last, into exclamations which were at once defiant, suppliant, despairing.

"No, Tom, no! I don't want your fortune. You know I don't! All this time you've been dangling it before my eyes, and all the time it's been a will-o'-the-wisp, leading me deeper and deeper into the mire. I was unhappy enough when first you came to me and spoke of it—but I've been unhappier since, a thousand times. You might have let me have it at the beginning, if you'd chosen—but you didn't choose. You used it to make of me a mock, and a gibe—your plaything—whipping boy! To-night the lure of it has only served as a means to bring us here together—she and I!—when you know I'd rather have gone a hundred miles barefooted to hide from her my face. I don't know if there is a fortune hidden in this house or not, and I don't care if behind its walls are concealed the riches of Golconda. I'll have none of it—it's too late! too late! I've asked you for what I'd give a many fortunes, and you've laughed at me. You'll not show, by so much as a sign, that you forgive her—now, at this eleventh hour. There's nothing else of yours I'll have."

In reply, there came again that quiet laughter, with in it that curious metallic quality, which seemed to act on the quivering nerves of the two sin-stained, wayworn wretches as if it had been molten metal. At the sound of it they gave a guilty start, as if the ghosts of all their sins had risen to scourge them.

From her demeanour, the laugher, diverting his attention from Ballingall, had apparently turned to address the woman. In accents which had grown perceptibly weaker since her first entering, she essayed to speak.

"Yes, Tom, I'll get up. If you wish me, Tom, of course I will. I'm—tired, Tom—that's all."

She did get up, in a fashion which demonstrated she was tired. The process of ascension was not the work of a moment, and when she had regained her feet, she swung this way and that, like a reed in the wind. It was only by what seemed a miracle that she did not fall.

"Don't be angry—I'm tired—Tom—that's all."

In her voice there was a weariness unspeakable.

Something, it seemed, was said to her—from which, as Ballingall had done, only in her feebler way, she expressed dissent.

"I don't want your money, Tom. It's so good of you; it's like you used to be, kind and generous. You always did give me lots of money, Tom, But—I don't want money—not now, Tom, not now."

Something else was said, which stung her, for she clasped her hands in front of her, with a movement of pain.

"I—didn't wish to make you angry, Tom—I'm—sure I didn't. Don't speak to me and look at me like that, don't, Tom, don't! You don't know how it hurts me, now—that I'm so tired. I'll go and fetch your money if you wish me—of course I will, if—you'll show me—where it is. I'll go at once. Upstairs? Yes, Tom—I don't think I'm—too tired to go upstairs, if—you'll come with me. Yes, Tom—I'm—going—now."

The woman turned towards the door hastily.

With a swift, eager gesture, in which there was something both mysterious and secretive, Ballingall addressed the four onlookers, the spellbound spectators of this, perhaps, unparelleled experience in the regions of experimental psychology. He spoke beneath his breath, hurriedly, hoarsely, w th fugitive sidelong glances, as if before all things he was anxious that what he said should be heard by them alone.

"He's going to show her where the fortune is!"

The woman opened the door.

CHAPTER XVII

THE KEY TO THE PUZZLE

She stood, for a second, with the handle of the open door in her grasp—as if she was glad of its support to aid her stand. Then, with a quick glance backwards, as of pleading to the one who exercised over her so strange a spell, she tottered from the room. She continued speaking as she went, as if deprecating the other's wrath.

"I shall be all right—in a moment—if you don't—hurry me at first. I'm only slow because—I'm a little tired. It'll soon go, this tired feeling, Tom—and I'll be sure—to be quicker when it's gone.'

Ballingall hung back as she passed from the room, seeming, from his attitude, to be in two minds whether to follow her at all. The others, as if taking their cue from him, seemed hesitating too—until Madge, with head thrown back, and fists hanging clenched at her sides, went after her through the door. Then they moved close on Madge's heels—Bruce Graham in front, Ballingall bringing up the rear.

The woman was staggering up the stairs, with obvious unwillingness—and, also, with more than sufficient feebleness. It was with difficulty she could lift her feet from step to step. Each time she raised her foot she gave a backward lurch, which threatened to precipitate her down the whole of the distance she had gained.

Madge's impulse was to dash forward, put her arms about the unfortunate creature's wrist and, if she needs must go forward, bear her bodily to the top of the stairs. But although, at the pitiful sight which the woman presented, her fingers tingled and her pulses throbbed, she was stayed from advancing to proffer her the assistance which she longed to render by the consciousness, against which she strove in vain, that between the woman and herself there was a something which not only did she dare not pass, but which she dare not even closely approach. Over and over again she told herself that it was nonsense—but a delusion born of the woman's diseased and conscience-haunted brain. There was absolutely nothing to be seen; and why should she, a healthy-minded young woman, suffer herself to be frightened by the vacant air? But in spite of all her efforts at self-persuasion, she allowed a considerable space to continue to exist between herself and the trembling wretch upon the stairs.

Slowly the queer procession advanced—the woman punctuating, as it were, with her plaintive wailings every step she took.

"Tom! Tom! Tom!" She continually repeated the name, with all the intonations of endearment, supplication, reproach, and even terror. To hear her was a liberal education in the different effects which may be produced by varieties of emphasis.

"Don't hurry me! I'm—going as quickly as I can. I—shall soon be at the top! It's so—so steep—a staircase—Tom."

At last the top was reached. She stood upon the landing, clinging to the banisters as she gasped for breath. Her figure swayed backward and forward, in so ominous a fashion that, halfway up the staircase, almost involuntarily Madge stretched out her arms to catch her if she fell. But she did not fall—nor was she allowed much time to recover from her exertions.

"I'm going—if—you'll let me—rest—for just one moment—Tom. Where do you wish me to go?"

It seemed as if her question was answered, for she gave a shuddering movement towards the wall, and burst into a passion of cries.

"No, Tom—not there! not there! not there! Don't make me go into our bedroom—not into our bedroom!"

The command which had been given her was apparently repeated, for, drawing herself away from the wall, she went with new and shuddering haste along the passage.

"I'm—I'm going! Only—have mercy—have mercy on me, Tom! I don't wish to anger you, only have mercy, Tom!"

The bedroom in front of the house was the one which was occupied by Ella. It was towards this room that the woman was moving with hurried, tremulous steps. Her unwillingness to advance was more marked than before, and yet she seemed urged by something which was both in front and behind her, which she was powerless to resist. They could see she shuddered as she went; and she uttered cries, half of terror, half of pain.

And yet she advanced with a decision, and a firmness, and also a rapidity, which was unlike anything she hitherto had shown. On the threshold of the room she stopped, starting back, and throwing out her hands in front of her.

"It's our bedroom, Tom—it's full of ghosts! Ghosts! Ghosts! Don't make me go into the bedroom, Tom."

But the propelling force, whatever it might have been, was beyond her power to withstand. She gave a sudden, exceeding bitter cry. Turning the handle, she flung the door right back upon its hinges. With a peal of laughter, which grated on the ears of those who heard almost more than anything which had gone before, she staggered into the room. As she disappeared they stopped, listening, with faces which had suddenly grown whiter, to her strange merriment.

"This is our bedroom—ha! ha! ha!—where you brought me when we were first married! Why, Tom, how many years is it since I was here? Ha, ha, ha!—I never thought I should come back to ou˙ bedroom, Tom—never! Ha, ha, ha!"

All at once there was a change in her tone—a note of terror. The laughter fled with the dreadful suddenness with which it had come.

"Don't, Tom, Don't! Have mercy—mercy! I'll do as you wish me—you know I will; I'll—get your money. Only—I didn't know—you kept it—in our bedroom—Tom. You didn't use to."

So soon as the laughter, fading, was exchanged for that panic cry, Madge hurried after her into the room—the others, as ever, hard upon her heels. The woman stood in the centre of the floor, looking about her with glances of evident bewilderment, as if seeking for something she had been told to look for. She searched in vain. Her eagerness was pitiful. She looked hither and thither, in every direction, as if, urged to the search, she feared, in speechless agony, the penalties of disobedience. All the while she kept giving short, sharp cries of strained and frenzied fear.

"I'm looking! I'm looking, Tom, as hard as I can, but—I see nothing—nothing, Tom! I'm doing as you tell me—I am—I am—I am! Oh, Tom, I am! But I don't see your money—I don't! I don't! If ycu'll show me where it is, I'll get it; but I see nothing of your money, Tom! Where is it?—Here!"

She moved towards the wash-hand stand, which was at the side of the room.

"Behind the washstand?"

She lifted the piece of furniture on one side with a degree of strength of which, light though it was, one would not have thought that she was capable. Getting behind it, she placed against the wall her eager, trembling hand.

"But—your money isn't here. There's nothing but the wall. Take the paper off the wall? But—how am I to do it?—With my fingers!—I can't tear off with my fingers, Tom. Oh, Tom, I'll try! Don't speak to me like that—I'll try!"

With feverish haste she dragged the apologies for gloves off her quivering hands.

"Where shall I tear it off?—Here? Yes, Tom, I'll try to tear it off just here."

Dropping on her knees she attacked with her nails the wall where, while she remained in that posture, it was about the height of her head—endeavouring to drive the edges through the paper, and to pick it off, as children do.

But her attempts were less successful than are the efforts of the average ingenious child.

"I can't, Tom, I can't! My fingers are not strong enough, and my nails are broken—don't be angry with me, Tom."

She made frantic little dabs at the wall. But her endeavours to make an impression on the paper were without result. It was plain that with her unassisted nails she might continue to peck at it in vain for ever.

Madge turned to Mr. Graham.

"Have you a pocket-knife?"

Without a word he took one from his waistcoat pocket.

Not waiting for him to open it, she took it from him with an action which almost amounted to a snatch. With her own fingers she opened the largest blade. Making a large, and under the circumstances curious circuit, in order to reach her, leaning over the washstand, touching the woman on the shoulder, she held out to her the knife.

Shrinking under Madge's finger, with an exclamation she looked round to see who touched her.

"Take this," said Madge. "It's a knife. With its help you'll be better able to tear the paper off the wall."

She took it—without a word of thanks, and, with it in her grasp, returned to the attack with energies renewed.

"I've got a knife, Tom, I've got a knife. Now I'll get the paper off quicker—much quicker. I'll soon get to your money, Tom."

But she did not get to it. On the contrary, the process of stripping off the paper did not proceed much more rapidly than before, even with the help of Mr. Graham's knife. It was with the greatest difficulty that she was able to get off two or three square inches.

The disappearance, however, of even this small portion revealed the fact that the paper-hanger who had been responsible for putting it into place, instead of stripping off the previous wall covering, as paperhangers are supposed to do, had been content, to save himself what he had, perhaps, deemed unnecessary trouble, to paste this latest covering on the previous one. This former paper appeared to have been of that old-fashioned kind which used to be popular in the parlours of country inns, and such-like places, and which was wont to be embellished with "pictorial illustrations." The scraping off, by the woman, of the small fragments of paper which she had succeeded in removing, showed that the one beneath it seemed to have been ornamented with more or less striking representations of various four-footed animals. On the space laid bare were figures of what might have been meant for anything; and which, in the light of the last line on Mr. Ballingall's manuscript, were probably intended for cats and dogs.

With these the woman was fumbling with hesitating, awkward fingers.

"Cat—dog? I don't—I don't understand, Tom—I see, Tom,—these are the pictures of cats and dogs. I'm blind, and stupid, and slow. I ought to have seen at once what they were?—I know I ought. But—be patient with me, Tom. Which one?—This one? Yes, I see—this one. It's—it's—yes, Tom, it's a dog's head, I see it is.—What am I to do with it? Press?—Yes, Tom, I am pressing.—Press harder? Yes, I'll—I'll try;

but I'm—I'm not very strong, and I can't press much harder. Have mercy!—have mercy, Tom! Say—say you forgive me—forgive me! but I—I can't press harder, Tom—I can't!"

She could not—so much was plain. Even as the words were passing from her lips, she relinquished pressing altogether. Uttering a little throbbing cry, she turned away from the wall, throwing up her arms with a gesture of entreaty, and sinking on to the floor, she lay there still. As she dropped, that gentle, mocking laugh rang through the startled room.

CHAPTER XVIII

MADGE APPLIES MORE STRENGTH

Was it imagination? Or was it fact? Did some one or something really pass from the room, causing in going a little current of air? With startled faces each put to the other an unspoken query.

Which none answered.

The woman lay there, motionless, her exceeding stillness seeming accentuated by the sudden silence which filled the room. Bruce Graham, moving forward, took her up in his arms, as if she were but a feather's weight. His knife fell from her nerveless fingers, tumbling to the floor with startling clatter. Madge picked it up. Her voice rang out with clarion clearness—the voice of a woman whose nerves were tense as fiddle-strings.

"I'll see if I cannot press harder. This mystery must be solved to-night—before some of us go mad; if pressing will do it, it shall soon be done—if there's strength in me at all."

There was strength in her—and not a little.

She went on her knees where the woman had been; and, as she had done, fumbled with her fingers where the paper had been scraped from the wall, peering closely at it, as she did so.

"A dog's head, is it?—it doesn't look as if it were a dog's head to me, and that's not because I'm stupid. It's to be pressed, is it?—Well, if pressing will do it, here's for pressing!"

She exerted all her force against the point to which the woman had been directed.

"It gives! It gives!—something gives beneath my thumb: it's the knob of a spring or something—I'm sure of it."

Turning, she looked up at Graham with flaming cheeks and flashing eyes.

"The spring is sure to be rusty. It will need all your strength. Try it again."

She tried again.

"It does give—it does! But whatever it is supposed to open is not likely to act now that the wall has been repapered. Some one go and fetch the hammer and the chisel from downstairs—we'll try another way."

She glanced at Jack, as if intending the suggestion to apply to him. But Ella clung to his arm, which perhaps prevented him from moving with the speed which might have been expected.

"Will no one go?" cried Madge. "Why, then, I'll go myself."

But that Bruce Graham would not permit. Swiftly depositing his still unconscious burden on Ella's bed, he went in search of the required tools, returning almost as soon as he had gone.

"I think, Miss Brodie, that perhaps you had better allow me to try my hand. I am stronger than you."

She gave way to him unhesitatingly.

"Drive the chisel into the wall and see if it is hollow."

He did as she bade him. A couple of blows put the thing beyond a doubt. The chisel disappeared up to the hilt through what was evidently but an outer shell. Madge continued to issue her instructions.

"Break the wall in! It's no use fumbling with dogs' head in search of hidden springs—with us it's a case of the shortest road's the best. Whatever's inside that wall has been there long enough to excuse us if we're a little neglectful of ceremonious observances."

In a few minutes the wall was broken in, the ancient woodwork offering no resistance to Bruce Graham's vigorous onslaught. A cavity was made large enough to thrust one's head in. Madge stopped him.

"That'll do—for the present! Now let's see what there is inside!"

She went down on her knees the better to enable her to see, Graham moving aside to give her room. She thrust her fair young face as far into the opening as she could get it—only to discover that she was obscuring her own light. Out it came again.

"Give me a light—a match, or something. It's as dark as pitch in there."

Graham gave her a box of matches. Striking one, she introduced it into what was as the heart of the wall.

"There is something in there!"

She dropped the match. Fortunately it went out as it fell.

"It's the hidden fortune!"

She gave a gasp. Then in an instant she was on her feet and was hastening towards the recumbent figure on the bed.

The woman still lay motionless. Madge, bending down, caught her by the shoulder, forgetful of all in her desire to impart the amazing news.

"Your husband's fortune's in the wall—we've found it there."

Something on the woman's face, in her utter stillness, seemed to fill her with new alarm. She called to the others.

"Ella!—Mr. Graham! Jack!" Her voice sank to a whisper; there was a catching of her breath. "Is she dead?"

They came hastening towards her. Jack Martyn, stopping halfway, looking round, startled them with a fresh inquiry, to which he himself supplied the answer.

"By George!—I say!—where's Ballingall?—Why, he's gone!"

CHAPTER XIX

THE WOMAN AND THE MAN

Yes—the woman was dead. Ballingall had gone—and the fortune was found.

Put in that way, it was a curious sequence of events.

Indeed, put in any way, there could be no doubt about the oddity of the part which the woman had played.

Medical examination clearly showed that death had come to her from natural causes. She must, the doctor said, have been within a hand's-breadth of death for, at any rate, the last twelve months. He declared that every vital organ was hopelessly diseased. Asked if the immediate cause of death was shock, he replied that there was nothing whatever in the condition of the body which could be regarded as supporting such a theory. In his opinion, the woman had burned out, like a candle, which, when it is all consumed, dies. Nothing, in his judgment, could have retarded the inevitable end; just as there was nothing to suggest that it came one instant sooner than might, in the natural course, have been expected.

That was what the doctor said in public, at the coroner's inquest.

He listened to them when, in private, they told him the strange story of the night's adventure, pronouncing at the conclusion an opinion which contained in it the essence of all wisdom, for it might be taken any way. The gist of it was this. Very probably for some time before her death, the woman had been light-headed. When people are light-headed they suffer from hallucinations. It was quite possible that, in her case, those hallucinations had taken the form—literally—of her injured husband. It was on record that hallucinations had taken form, in similar cases. It was a perfectly feasible and reasonable theory which supposed that the woman, wandering, a homeless outcast, in the streets of London, delirious, premonitions of her approaching dissolution being borne in upon her in spite of her delirium, would turn her dying footsteps towards her one-time home, to which, as her behaviour in forcing herself on Madge plainly showed, her thoughts had recently returned. Nor, under the circumstances, was there anything surprising in her delusion that her husband had led her there.

It was when asked to explain how it was that she had hit upon the hiding-place of her husband's fortune—hit upon it, as it seemed, altogether against her will, that the doctor became oracular. But even here he was not without his hints as to the direction in which an explanation might be found.

He pointed out that our study of the science of mental psychology was still in its infancy. But, even so far as it had gone, it seemed to suggest the possibility of what has come to be called telepathic communication between two minds—even when the whilom owner of one of the minds has passed beyond the confines of the grave. This sounded a trifle abstruse. But as the doctor professed his inability to put it any clearer, they had to take his statement as it stood, and make out just as much of it as they were able.

As for Ballingall's pretensions to having shared the woman's hallucination—if hallucination it was—the doctor pooh-poohed them altogether. The man was as mad as the woman, and madder; and an impudent rogue to boot. Where was he? Let him come forward, and allow himself and his statements to be scientifically tested. Then it would be shown what reliance could be placed on anything which he might say.

But where Ballingall was, was exactly the problem which they found insoluble. He had vanished as completely as if he had never existed. The presumption was, that while they had been absorbed in watching Madge's efforts to carry on the work of discovery from the point at which the woman had left it, he had sneaked, unnoticed, from the room and from the house. The curious feature was that they were unable to agree as to the exact moment at which he could have gone. Bruce Graham declared that he was in the room when he went to fetch the hammer and chisel, and that he was still there when he returned. Madge protested that he was in the room when she ran across to the recumbent figure on Ella's bed. If so, since Jack discovered his absence within less than a minute afterwards, it was during that scant sixty seconds that he made good his escape.

Why he had gone at all was difficult to say. One might have thought that after what he had undergone during his search for the fortune he would hardly have disappeared at the moment of its finding. He had suffered so much in looking, that he had earned at least a share, when at last it was brought to light. Such, certainly, was the strong feeling of its actual discoverer. He stood in need enough of money; that was sure. Why then, at what from one point of view might be described as the very moment of his triumph, had he vanished?

He alone could tell.

They could only give wild guesses. Nothing has been seen or heard of him from that hour to this. They put advertisements for him in the papers, without result. Then, as they felt that living the sort of life which he probably was living—that is, if he was living at all—it was within the range of probability that a newspaper would never come his way, and that he would never glance at it if it did, they distributed handbills broadcast through the slums of London, beseeching him to apply to a certain address, and offering a reward to any one who could give an account of his proceedings after the night on which he had taken himself away.

To those handbills they did receive answers—in abundance. There were evidently plenty of people who were willing, nay, anxious, to lay their hands on that reward, just as there seemed several Charles Ballingalls with whom they were acquainted. But no one of them was the Charles Ballingall. More than once they thought they had chanced on him at last; the stories told were such very specious ones, and they followed up the trail till it proved beyond all manner of doubt to be a false one. When the Charles Ballingall to whom it referred was unearthed, he proved, in each and every case, to be not in the least like theirs.

And so the presumption is that the man is dead. He was, probably, as the doctor suggested, more than half out of his mind on that eventful night; his sins had brought him suffering enough to have driven the average mortal mad. It is not unlikely that the strange things which then transpired, completing the work of destruction, robbed him of his few remaining senses; and that, at that last moment, when Madge Brodie announced her discovery of what he had sought with so much pain and with such ardour, the irony of fate which seemed to have pursued him, pressing on him still, had driven him out into the night, a raving lunatic, seeking anywhere and anyhow for escape from the burden of life which haunted him.

God alone can tell where and how he found it.

CHAPTER XX

And the fortune?

This remark may be made—that had they not found it when they did there would very shortly have been nothing left to find. Mr. Thomas Ossington had chosen for the treasure-chest a simple opening in the wall, to which access had originally been gained by touching a spring. This spring had been concealed under what had probably been a picture of a dog's head; the fifth alternating dog's head on the right-hand side of the bedroom door. When you pressed it a door flew open. But this primitive treasure-chest, if not entirely obvious to the world at large, was open to the rats and mice, and similar small deer, who had their happy hunting-grounds within the wall itself. The result was that, when the contents were examined, it was found that the bundles of bank-notes had been gnawed, in some cases to unrecognisable shreds; that meals—hearty ones of the cut-and-come-again description—had been made of parchment deeds, bonds, share certificates, and similar impediments; that coin—gold coin—had been contained in bags, which bags had been consumed, even to the strings which once had tied them. The coins lay under accumulations of dust, in heaps upon the floor. On several were actually well-marked indentations, showing that sharp, gleaming teeth had applied to them a stringent test before finally deciding that they really were not good to eat. A curious spectacle the whole presented when first brought to the light of day.

However, in but few cases had the damage proceeded to lengths which had rendered what was left absolutely worthless—discovery had come just in the nick of time. The Bank of England was good enough to hand over cash in exchange for the fragments of all notes of which there was satisfactory evidence that there had been once a whole. The various documents which represented property were none of them in a condition which rendered recognition altogether impossible, and when it was once established what they were, for all intents and purposes they were as available for their original use as if they had been in a condition of pristine freshness.

Altogether the find represented a sum of something like £40,000. Not a large fortune, as fortunes go, but still a comfortable capital to be the possessor of. If fate only had been kind to him, and the men and women who formed his world of finer texture, Tom Ossington might have been as happy as the days were long.

Oddly enough, the real trouble came after the fortune was found. The difficulty was as to whom it belonged—not because the claimants were so many, but because they were so few.

It was Madge's wish that it should be divided between those who were actually present at the moment of its discovery, maintaining that such a division would be in accordance with both law and equity. Ballingall's continued disappearance resolved the number of these into four—Ella, Jack Martyn, Bruce Graham, and herself. The first rift in the lute was caused by Mr. Graham, he refusing point-blank to have part or parcel in any such transaction. He maintained that the fortune had been found by Madge, and that therefore, in accordance with the terms of the will, the whole of it was hers. In any case he would have none of it. He had felt, on mature reflection, that Ballingall's accusations had not been without foundation, that his conduct had been unprofessional, that he had had no right to share his confidence with anybody—that, in short, he had behaved ill in the whole affair; and that, therefore, he had no option but to decline to avail himself of any advantages which were, so to speak, the proceeds of his misbehaviour.

When she heard this, Madge laughed outright. Seeing that her laughter made no impression, and that the gentleman continued of the same opinion still, she was moved to use language which was, to say the least, surprising. It was plain that, beneath the lash of the lady's tongue, he was unhappy. But his unhappiness did not go deep enough to induce him to change his mind. When it was obvious that his resolve was adamant, and that by no means could he be induced to move from it, she announced her own decision.

"Very well; if the fortune's mine, it's mine. And if it's mine I can do what I like with it. And what I like, is to divide it with Ella; and if Ella will not have half, then I'll not have a farthing either. And the whole shall go to the Queen, or to whoever unclaimed money does go. And you'll find that I can be as firm—or as obstinate—as anybody else."

"But, my dear," observed Ella, mildly, "I never said that I wouldn't have half. I'm sure I'll be delighted. I'll need no pressing—and thank you very kindly, ma'am."

"I do believe, Ella," returned Madge, with calmness which was both significant and deadly, "that you are the only reasonable person with whom I am acquainted."

So it was arranged—the two girls divided the whole; which of course meant, as Madge knew perfectly, that Jack Martyn would have his share. As a matter of fact, Mr. and Mrs. Martyn have been husband and wife for some time now, and are doing very well.

And it is said—as such things are said—that Madge Brodie will be Mrs. Bruce Graham yet before she dies. It is believed by those who know them best that he would give his eyes to marry her, and that she has made up her mind to marry him.

This being so, it would seem as if a marriage might ensue.

If such is the case, it appears extremely likely, if Madge ever is his wife, that, whether he will or won't, Bruce Graham will have to have his share.

She is as obstinate as he is—every whit.

Richard Bernard Heldmann was born on 12th October 1857, in St Johns Wood, North London, to parents Joseph Heldmann and Emma Marsh.

Shortly after his birth his father became ensnared in a bankruptcy proceedings which enforced the abandonment of a career as a merchant for that of a schoolmaster at a school in Hammersmith, West London.

By his early 20's the young Heldmann, showing a talent for writing, began publishing fiction. In 1880, he began to publish works of boys' school and adventure stories for the myriad magazine publications all eager for good well-written content. The most important of these was Union Jack, one of the better quality boys' weekly magazine associated with the popular authors G. A. Henty and W.H.G. Kingston.

Heldmann was promoted to co-editor in October 1882, but his association with the publication ended suddenly in June 1883. After this, Heldmann published no further fiction under that name.

The reason at the time was not immediately apparent but in April 1884 Heldmann was sentenced to 18 months of hard labour for issuing a series of cheques, all forged, in France and Britain the year before.

In order to be well away from the scandal and damage this had caused to his reputation Heldmann adopted a pseudonym on his release from jail. Shortly thereafter the name 'Richard Marsh' began to appear in the literary periodicals. The use of his mother's maiden name seems both a release from the criminal record now associated with his given name and a lifeline to a fresh beginning.

A stroke of very good fortune arrived when his novel The Beetle was published in 1897. There had been more than a few previous publications of his works but The Beetle would turn out to be his greatest commercial success and added some much-needed gravitas to his literary reputation. The story concerns a mysterious oriental person who follows a British politician to London, and then wreaks havoc with his powers of hypnosis and shape-shifting. The Beetle has some similar aspects to certain other novels of the period, including those such as Bram Stoker's Dracula, George du Maurier's Trilby, and Sax Rohmer's many Fu Manchu novels. Like Dracula, and also the sensation novels written by Wilkie Collins and others during the 1860s, The Beetle is narrated from the various viewpoints of multiple characters to create suspense. The novel is also layered with many themes and issues of the Victorian era including women's rights, unemployment, urban poverty, radical politics, homosexuality, science, and Britain's imperial adventures, particularly in regard to Egypt and the Sudan. The Beetle sold out upon its initial print run and thereafter sold well for the next several decades. After Marsh's early death the novel's story was made into a film and adapted for the London stage, both in the 1920's.

It should also be noted that in the year of its first publication it outsold Dracula, then also in its first year of publication. In hindsight a remarkable achievement.

Marsh was a prolific writer and wrote almost 80 volumes of fiction as well as many short stories, across several genres from horror and crime to romance and humour.

However, at horror he was particularly adept. Works such as The Goddess: A Demon (1900), in which an Indian sacrificial idol comes to life with murderous resolve, and The Joss: A Reversion (1901), whose central premise is that of an Englishman who transforms himself into a hideous oriental idol are prime examples.

An important element of many of Marsh's novels is the investigation of the mystery. Several of his novels are centered on the crime and its subsequent detection. In the novel Philip Bennion's Death (1897) a bachelor is discovered dead the day after discussing Thomas De Quincey's essay on murder as a fine art, and his neighbour and friend begin efforts to solve his death. In The Datchet Diamonds (1898) a young man who has lost a fortune on the stock market mistakenly swaps bags with a diamond thief, and then find himself pursued by both the thieves and police. In A Spoiler of Men (1905), Marsh puts together crime and science-fiction; the gentleman-criminal villain renders people slaves to his will by a chemical injection.

As with many authors success with popular fiction was never quite enough. He also wanted to be regarded as a serious author. His novel A Second Coming (1900) imagines Christ's return to an early-20th century London and is his most well-handled attempt in that pursuit.

His prolific output of short stories ensured his being published in a plethora of magazines including Household Words, Cornhill Magazine, The Strand Magazine, and Belgravia, as well as in a number of short story book collections. These collections; The Seen and the Unseen (1900), Marvels and Mysteries (1900), Both Sides of the Veil (1901) and Between the Dark and the Daylight (1902) all feature an eclectic mix of humour, crime, romance and the occult.

He also published several serial short stories. Here he was able to develop characters whose adventures could be related in discrete stories across numerous editions of a magazine. An example is Mr. Pugh and Mr. Tress of Curios (1898). They are rival collectors between whom pass a series of bizarre and disturbing objects—poisoned rings, pipes which seem to come to life, a phonograph record on which a murdered woman seems to speak from the dead, and the severed hand of a 13th-century aristocrat.

During his career he sometimes came up with characters or stories ahead of their time. His character Miss Judith Lee, a young teacher of deaf pupils whose lip-reading ability involves her with mysteries that she solves by acting as a detective was very pro-active in this regard.

Richard Marsh died from heart disease in Haywards Heath in Sussex on 9th August 1915.

Several of his novels were published posthumously.

As Bernard Heldmann
Boxall School: A Tale of Schoolboy Life (1881)
Dorrincourt [Union Jack, April-September 1881]
Expelled: Being the Story of a Young Gentleman (1882)
Daintree (1883)

As Richard Marsh
Capturing a Convict (Strand Magazine 1893)
The Devil's Diamond (1893)
The Mahatma's Pupil (1893)
The Strange Wooing of Mary Bowler (1895)
Mrs Musgrave—and her Husband (1895)
The Mystery of Philip Bennion's Death (1897)
The Crime and the Criminal (1897)
The Duke and the Damsel (1897)
The Beetle: A Mystery (1897)
The House of Mystery (1898)
Under One Cover: Eleven Stories by S. Baring-Gould, Richard Marsh, Ernest G. Henham, Fergus Hume,
Andrew Merry and A. St John Adcock (1898)
Curios: Some Strange Adventures of Two Bachelors (1898)
Tom Ossington's Ghost (1898)
The Datchet Diamonds (1898)
The Woman with One Hand and Mr Ely's Engagement (1899)
In Full Cry (1899)
Frivolities: Especially Addressed to Those Who Are Tired of Being Serious (1899)
The Purse Which Was Found
For One Night Only
Returning a Verdict
The Chancellor's Ward
A Honeymoon Trip
The Burglar's Blunder
Ninepence
A Battlefield Up-to-date
Mr. Harland's Pupils
A Burglar Alarm
A Lesson in Sculling
Outside
The Chase of the Ruby (1900)
An Aristocratic Detective (1900)
A Hero of Romance (1900)
The Seen and the Unseen (1900)
The Goddess: A Demon (1900)
Ada Vernham, Actress (1900)
A Second Coming (1900)
Marvels and Mysteries (1900)
The Long Arm of Coincidence
The Mask

An Experience
Pourquoipas
By Suggestion
A Silent Witness
To Be Used Against Him
The Words of a Little Child
How He Passed!
The Joss: A Reversion (1901)
Both Sides of the Veil (1901)
Amusement Only (1901)
The Twickenham Peerage (1902)
Between the Dark and the Daylight (1902)
The Adventures of Augustus Short: Things Which I Have Done for Others and Wish I Hadn't (1902)
A Metamorphosis (1903)
The Death Whistle (1903)
The Magnetic Girl (1903)
Miss Arnott's Marriage (1904)
Garnered (1904)
A Duel (1904)
A Spoiler of Men (1905)
The Marquis of Putney (1905)
The Confessions of a Young Lady (1905)
Under One Flag (1906)
In the Service of Love (1906)
The Garden of Mystery (1906)
A Woman Perfected (1907)
The Romance of a Maid of Honour (1907)
The Girl and the Miracle (1907)
The Surprising Husband (1908)
The Coward behind the Curtain (1908)
That Master of Ours (1908)
A Royal Indiscretion (1909)
The Interrupted Kiss (1909)
The Girl in the Blue Dress (1909)
The Lovely Mrs Blake (1910)
Live Men's Shoes (1910)
The Twin Sisters (1911)
A Drama of the Telephone (1911)
Violet Forster's Lover (1912)
Sam Briggs: His Book (1912)
Judith Lee: Some Pages from her Life (1912)
The Master of Deception (1913)
Justice—Suspended (1913)
If It Please You (1913)
The Woman in the Car (1914)
Molly's Husband (1914)
Margot—and her Judges (1914)
The Man with Nine Lives (1915)

Love in Fetters (1915)
His Love or his Life (1915)
The Flying Girl (1915)
Violet Forster's Lover (1916)
The Adventures of Judith Lee (1916)
Sam Briggs, V.C. (1916)
Coming of Age (1916)
The Great Temptation (1916)
The Deacon's Daughter (1917)
On the Jury (1918)
Orders to Marry ([1918)
Outwitted (1919)
Apron-Strings (1920)

Periodicals

For Debt, Windsor Magazine (January 1902)
Returning a Verdict, Cornhill Magazine (January 1896)
The Lost Duchess, Cornhill Magazine (January 1895)
Mrs Riddles Daughter, All the Year Round (17 March 1894)
An Episcopal Scandal, Cornhill Magazine (February 1894)
A Rubber or Two, All the Year Round (16 September 1893)
A First Night, Cornhill Magazine (April 1893)
The Mystery of Philip Bennion's Death, Household Words (3/10/17/24/31 December 1892)
The Princess Margaretta, Household Words (3 December 1892)
The Puzzle, Cornhill Magazine (November 1892)
A Victim to Art, All the Year Round (2 July 1892)
The Burglar's Blunder, Derby Mercury (24 June 1891)
Pourquoipas, All the Year Round (9/16 May 1891)
The Pipe, Cornhill Magazine (March 1891)
When Greek Joined Greek, Household Words (6 September 1890)
His First Experiment, Cornhill Magazine (September 1890)
"Mignonette", All the Year Round (9 August 1890)
The Long Arm of Coincidence, Household Words (24 May 1890)
The Match of the Season, Cornhill Magazine (May 1890)
A Set of Chessmen, Cornhill Magazine (April 1890)
A Dream of Diamonds, Household Words (7 December 1889)
My Uncle's Flirtation, Household Words (16 November 1889)
"Em", Household Words (2 November 1889)
The Barnes Mystery: An Adventure of Judith Lee, Strand Magazine (October 1916)
"Scandalous!", Strand Magazine (August 1916)
What Fell on her Hat, Strand Magazine (April 1916)
The Adventures of Sam Briggs: On the Film, Strand Magazine (March 1916)
A Set of Chessmen, Cassell's Magazine of Fiction and Popular Literature (Dec 1915)
Sam Briggs Becomes a Soldier: A Fighting Man, Strand Magazine (December 1915)
Sam Briggs Becomes a Soldier: On the Way Home, Strand Magazine (November 1915)

Sam Briggs Becomes a Soldier: An Official Mistake, Strand Magazine (October 1915)

Sam Briggs Becomes a Soldier: In their Own Gas, Strand Magazine (September 1915)

Sam Briggs Becomes a Soldier: Sanctuary, Strand Magazine (August 1915)

Sam Briggs Becomes a Soldier: In the Nick of Time, Strand Magazine (July 1915)

Sam Briggs Becomes a Soldier: A Night Surprise for the Germans, Strand Magazine (June 1915)

Sam Briggs Becomes a Soldier: In the Trenches, Strand Magazine (May 1915)

Sam Briggs Becomes a Soldier: Baptism of Fire, Strand Magazine (April 1915)

Sam Briggs Becomes a Soldier: Two Stripes, Strand Magazine (March 1915)

Life in the King's New Army: Jack Carpenter's True Story, VI: Career for our Boys, Daily Mail (27 February 1915)

Life in the King's New Army: Jack Carpenter's True Story, V: The Tailor and the Man, Daily Mail (26 February 1915)

Life in the King's New Army: Jack Carpenter's True Story, IV: Hutments', Daily Mail (25 February 1915)

Life in the King's New Army: Jack Carpenter's True Story, III: First-Rate Fighting Men', Daily Mail (24 February 1915)

Life in the King's New Army: Jack Carpenter's True Story, II: The Berwick Borderers, Daily Mail (23 February 1915)

Life in the King's New Army: Jack Carpenter's True Story, I: Crossed Swords, Daily Mail (22 February 1915)

Sam Briggs Becomes a Soldier: A Man in the Making, Strand Magazine (February 1915)

Sam Briggs Becomes a Soldier: Sam Briggs Becomes a Soldier, Strand Magazine (January 1915)

The Amazing Visitor, Strand Magazine (December 1914)

Looping the Loop: An Adventure of Sam Briggs, Strand Magazine (August 1914)

The Torch, Strand Magazine (October 1913)

"Gaiety" Abroad, Strand Magazine (September 1913), 274-82

A Self-Appointed Guardian, English Illustrated Magazine (August 1913)

For the Cause, Strand Magazine (April 1913)

The Adventures of Judith Lee: The Affair of the Montagu Diamonds, Strand Magazine (February 1913)

The Adventures of Judith Lee: Mandragora, Strand Magazine (August 1912)

The Adventures of Judith Lee: "8 Elm Grove—Back Entrance", Strand Magazine (July 1912)

The Adventures of Judith Lee: The Restaurant Napolitain, Strand Magazine (June 1912)

The Adventures of Judith Lee: Uncle Jack, Strand Magazine (May 1912)

The Adventures of Judith Lee: Was It by Chance Only? Strand Magazine (April 1912)

The Adventures of Judith Lee: Isolda, Strand Magazine (March 1912)

The Adventures of Judith Lee: "Auld Lang Syne", Strand Magazine (January 1912)

The Adventures of Judith Lee: The Miracle, Strand Magazine (December 1911)

The Adventures of Judith Lee: Matched

The Burglary in Berkeley Square, Pearson's Magazine (December 1908)

The River of Light, Strand Magazine (December 1908)

The Girl in the Light Blue Dress, Strand Magazine (October 1908)

O'Rourke of the Saucy Sixth, Grand Magazine (June 1908)

The Adventures of Sam Briggs: The Limerick, Strand Magazine (February 1908)

The Adventures of Sam Briggs: The Star of Romance, Strand Magazine (July 1907)

The Adventures of Sam Briggs: A Social Evening, Strand Magazine (April 1907)

My Best Story and Why I Think So No. 21: The Strange Occurrences in Canterstone Gaol, Grand Magazine (October 1906)

The Adventures of Sam Briggs: That Hansom, Strand Magazine (May 1906)

The Adventures of Sam Briggs: Her Fourth, Strand Magazine (December 1905)

The Adventures of Sam Briggs: A Modest Half-Crown, Strand Magazine (November 1905)

The Adventures of Sam Briggs: The Gift Horse, Strand Magazine (March 1905)

My Wedding Day, Strand Magazine (January 1905)

The Adventures of Sam Briggs: The Girl on the Sands, Strand Magazine (October 1904)

The Parson, the Soldier, and the Child, London Magazine (November 1903)

The Girl and the Boy, London Magazine (October 1903)

By Whose Hand? New Short Novel by Richard Marsh, Answers (1 August – 31 October 1903)

A Girl Who Couldn't, Strand Magazine (January 1903)

The Kit-Bag, Windsor Magazine, 17 (January 1903), 298-309

Their Reasons: Two Hitherto Unreported Conversations, House Annual (1902)

At Large: Being the Strange Perils and Experiences of George Otway, Suspect, Answers (12 July - 27 December 1902)

The Handwriting, Strand Magazine (June 1902)

La Haute Finance, Windsor Magazine (March 1902)

A Wonderful Girl, Strand Magazine (March 1902)

Skittles, English Illustrated Magazine, (February/March 1902)

Breaking the Ice, Strand Magazine (February 1902)

My Aunt's Excursion, Windsor Magazine (January 1902)

The Haunted Chair: The Story of a Strange Mystery, Harmsworth London Magazine (January 1902)

Miss Donne's Great Gamble, Strand Magazine (November 1901)

The Man in the Glass Cage; or The Strange Story of the Twickenham Peerage, Manchester Times, (6 September – 27 December 1901

The Adventures of Augustus Short: Things Which I Have Done for Others, and Wish I Hadn't: The Address Which I Gave for Rudman, Cassell's Magazine (November 1901)

The Adventures of Augustus Short: Things Which I Have Done for Others, and Wish I Hadn't: Jones's Love Affair, Cassell's Magazine (October 1901)

The Adventures of Augustus Short: Things Which I Have Done for Others, and Wish I Hadn't: The Duel I Fought of Jarvis, Cassell's Magazine (September 1901)

The Adventures of Augustus Short: Things Which I Have Done for Others, and Wish I Hadn't: Griffin's Offspring, Cassell's Magazine (August 1901)

The Adventures of Augustus Short: Things Which I Have Done for Others, and Wish I Hadn't: McCulloch's Shoes, Cassell's Magazine (July 1901)

The Adventures of Augustus Short: Things Which I Have Done for Others, and Wish I Hadn't: The Fitzroy-Jenkinsons' Rooms, Cassell's Magazine (June 1901)

Staggers, Windsor Magazine (April 1901)

How I Drove a Motor Car for Randal, Strand Magazine (April 1901)

The Disappearance of Mrs Macrecham: The Amazing Story of a Strange Cat, Harmsworth Monthly Pictorial Magazine (March 1901)

The Irregularity of the Juryman, Strand Magazine (December 1900)

The Strange Fortune of Pollie Blythe: The Story of a Chinese "God", Manchester Times (12 October 1900 – 8 February 1901)

Pugh's Poisoned Ring, Harmsworth Monthly Pictorial Magazine (October 1900)

Willyum, Penny Illustrated Paper and Illustrated Times, (26 May 1900)

Willyum, Hampshire Telegraph and Naval Chronicle (26 May 1900)

The Goddess: A Demon, Manchester Times (12 January – 30 March 1900)

The Stolen Treaty, Manchester Times (27 October 1899)

For One Night Only, Answers (8 April 1899)

In Full Cry, Manchester Times (3 March – 9 June 1899)

The Colonel's Cane, Cassell's Magazine (February 1899)

The Burglary at Azalea Villa, Manchester Times, (13 January 1899)

The Burglary at Azalea Villa, Newcastle Weekly Courant (14 January 1899)

Our Christmas Burglar, Answers (17 December 1898)

Something to his Advantage, Manchester Times (7 October – 4 November 1898)

A Lesson in Sculling, Newcastle Weekly Courant (October 1898)

That Five Hundred Pound Price, Harmsworth Monthly Pictorial Magazine (September 1898)

The Chancellor's Ward, Harmsworth Monthly Pictorial Magazine (August 1898)

The Ossington Mystery, Ipswich Journal (1 April – 17 June 1898)

The Duchess of Datchet's Diamonds, New Zealand Graphic and Ladies' Journal (New Zealand) (7 May – 25 June 1898)

The Peril of Paul Lessingham: The Story of a Haunted Man, Answers (13 March – 19 June 1897)

The Purse Which Was Found, Answers (17 April 1897)

The Rector and the Curate, Answers (19 December 1896)

An Illustration of Modern Science, Pall Mall Magazine (November 1896)

A Battlefield Up-to-Date, Idler Magazine (August 1896)

Twins, Idler Magazine (January 1896)

Lady Wishaw's Hand, Leeds Mercury (January 1895)

Young George, St Nicholas (March 1894)

Exchange Is Robbery, Idler Magazine (December 1893 - January 1894)

The Tipster: An Impossible Story, Home Chimes (December 1893)

The Influence of Women, Home Chimes (November 1893)

By Deputy: A Reminiscence of Travel, Home Chimes (October 1893)

Rivals, Home Chimes (September 1893)

Capturing a Convict, Strand Magazine (August 1893)

A Burglar Alarm, Home Chimes (June 1893)

Music Halls and Theatres, Home Chimes (March 1893)

A Strange Bride, Manchester Times (6/13 January 1893)

The Mask, Gentleman's Magazine (December 1892)

A Vision of the Night, Strand Magazine (December 1892)

Nelly, Home Chimes (November 1892)

A Prophet: A Story, New England Magazine (October - November 1892)

Mr Harland's Pupils, Home Chimes (August 1892)

The Brothers in Grey, Home Chimes (April 1892)

The Half-Back, Derby Mercury (March 1892)

The Half-Back, Home Chimes (February 1892)

The Violin, Home Chimes (December 1891)

The Short Story, Home Chimes (August 1891)

Magical Music, Gentleman's Magazine (May 1891)

A Honeymoon Trip, Home Chimes (April 1891)

Mitwaterstraand, Time (September 1890)

A Pack of Cards, Longman's Magazine (August 1890)

The Burglar's Blunder, Ladies' Journal (Canada) (1 July 1890)

The Strange Occurrences in Canterstone Jail, Blackwood's Edinburgh Magazine (June 1890)

A Substitute: The Story of My Last Cricket-Match, Longman's Magazine (June 1890)

The Burglar's Blunder, Gentleman's Magazine (May 1890)

A Silent Witness, Belgravia (October 1889)

A Bed for the Night, Belgravia (Summer 1889)

Payment for a Life, Belgravia (Summer 1888)

www.ingramcontent.com/pod-product-compliance
Lightning Source LLC
Chambersburg PA
CBHW071409170626
46811CB00003B/1322